AND MY SEE-THROUGH HEART

AND MY SEE-THROUGH HEART

by Véronique Ovaldé

TRANSLATED BY ADRIANA HUNTER

Portobello
BOOKS

Published by Portobello Books Ltd 2009

Portobello Books Ltd
Twelve Addison Avenue
Holland Park
London
W11 4QR, UK

First published in France as *Et mon coeur transparent* by
Editions de l'Olivier in 2008

A CIP catalogue record is available from the British Library

9 8 7 6 5 4 3 2 1

ISBN 978 1 84627 181 6

www.portobellobooks.com

Designed in Minion by Dorothy Carico Smith
Typeset by Avon DataSet Ltd, Bidford on Avon, Warwickshire

Printed in the UK by CPI William Clowes Beccles NR34 7TL

PART ONE

ONE

Lancelot's wife died tonight.

When, on the day they met, he told her, My name's Lancelot, he said it in such an apologetic, such a contrite way that she was won over. She replied, Well, that's not a problem, I'll call you Paul. And she burst out laughing when he told her his surname was Rubinstein. Lancelot Rubinstein. He felt both put out and delighted by the way his wife – who was not yet his wife – laughed. She had a bouncing laugh, a laugh that pinged off smooth surfaces and was reflected everywhere. Lancelot Rubinstein thought he would find it hard getting by without it from now on. This was to do with the fact that it was warm and woolly. That is what he thought that first evening, the evening of the day he met his wife. Lancelot was a man who could think of a laugh as warm and woolly.

So tonight Lancelot lost his wife who called him Paul.

The night that marks the beginning of Lancelot's mourning is an arctic one, a night of blizzards and black ice.

Lancelot and his wife live in Catano, a rather isolated town not far from Milena. A sort of elastic suburb. Milena is the most interesting city for many kilometres around; it has a university, bars that are open on Sundays, drugs, grocery shops (not just huge supermarkets you can only reach by car), a festival of short films, and two theatres, one of which is devoted entirely to animal puppets. Milena is in the middle of an area that is cold virtually all year round, with the worst bouts in February. There are still bears and wolves in the forests around Catano, and local poachers are most likely to trap white hares, ermine and arctic foxes. All creatures whose pelts they can sell off in Milena. There are people there who know what to do with them and will buy them at exorbitant prices.

Lancelot is not asleep tonight. He is sitting in his favourite armchair in latticework leather, with fake zebra-skin cushions for his head. When the telephone rings he is watching a programme about Thomson's gazelles that he recorded earlier and put on in the background. Shit, he thinks with a scowl, they really should think before calling at this time of night, it could wake the children.

The children he is worrying about at this point are imaginary ones.

Lancelot and his wife do not have any children. Despite this incontestable truth, when the inopportune phone rings, his very first thought is for his imaginary children. He frowns, scolds himself and picks up.

Hello?

Lancelot Rubinstein? (There is quite a degree of uncertainty in the caller's voice as he says this name, and the voice actually reminds Lancelot of someone, Robert Mitchum perhaps?)

Yes.

Milena Police Department.

Oh? (Now Lancelot wonders, is he sure he remembered to renew his fishing permit, has he still got any cannabis in the toolbox on the shelves at the back of the garage and did he definitely renew his car insurance?)

It's about your wife.

My wife?

You do have a wife?

Yes, yes, of course, I was on the phone to her just quarter of an hour ago.

You need to get to the Omoko bridge right away.

Why?

Your wife's had an accident.

At the Omoko bridge?

Yes.

That's impossible. It's not my wife. Quarter of an hour ago my wife was at the airport waiting for her flight (Lancelot wriggles deeper into his latticework leather armchair and takes one of the fake zebra-skin cushions to hold over his stomach). I took her there myself this evening.

Is your wife called Irina Rubinstein?

Yes (Lancelot takes a second cushion, then a third, piling up layers of protection over his abdomen).

Well, I advise you to come as quickly as possible before we manage to get her out of the vehicle and take her... (the man hesitates, gives a little cough) to hospital? (He does not sound very sure that this is where Irina Rubinstein will be transferred to.)

Lancelot swallows hard and hugs his shield of false zebra skin close to him, he can feel panic starting to creep over him, beginning with the tips of his fingers, he feels it very specifically taking hold of the pads of his fingers and working its way up his nerves, he'd like to curb the process but the panic is right there, permeating his whole body and mind, lodging itself brutally in his sternum like an uppercut, he can't breathe any more, his field of vision shrinks (Am I going to pass out? he wonders), then expands again.

He says, I'm coming. But no sound comes from his mouth. So he clears his throat and articulates, I'm coming. He is not absolutely sure Robert Mitchum heard him but that doesn't matter. Lancelot hangs up, gets to his feet, grabs the car keys, goes down to the garage, and sets off, launching into the dark and the snow. He forgets to worry about his imaginary children. All he can do is rush to be with Irina, his star, his treasure, his light, all he can do is try to ward off what he suspects has already happened by saying, No no no no no, over and over again, as if to convince himself, saying it through clenched teeth, and the rhythm of it becomes another thrumming in his body. He sets off, clinging closely to the steering wheel to make himself go faster and help him see through the snow, which is coiling and swirling with indecent exuberance, Lancelot would love to go even faster and invert the course of time to suspend the onset of the drama that has erupted into his life and, he can tell, will now take up every millimetre of space.

TWO

When Lancelot met Irina he was already married.

But every day spent with his wife Elisabeth left him more perplexed, what could he be doing with her and what can he have thought he would achieve with her?

Elisabeth was a primary-school teacher and, over the years spent practising that profession, had adopted a very particular way of addressing people. She seemed to confuse adults she came across with the children she was responsible for in class. For example, she would ask Lancelot, Could you make that delicious chocolate cake (pronouncing her request with excessive gaps between the syllables as if dictating it to him, and grimacing with effort so she seemed to be performing complicated exercises to minimize wrinkles), but obviously without any rum in it, and could you please cut it (here she mimed with an invisible knife in her right hand) into equal parts to make it easier for the little ones?

Lancelot looked at her, wondered what he was doing

with her, and made his delicious chocolate cake for the school fair.

Lancelot stayed at home all day correcting proofs. He sat down at his desk early in the morning, just after Elisabeth left, and started work, breaking off at about eleven thirty to make a sandwich; he turned on the radio, listened to the topical comedy show of the day, switched off the radio, and stood by the window to eat his sandwich full of gherkins (they stimulated his palate and made him salivate), watching what was going on in the tree out in the courtyard. A great deal went on in that camphor tree. It was utterly exceptional. At the time Lancelot and his wife lived in a very large town called Camerone, and the fact that a tree like that had managed to survive toxic attacks, bombings in the last war and the strange viruses that had decimated the camphor tree population in the area was in itself a miracle. Lancelot could gaze at his miraculous camphor tree for hours. Several cats lived in it (he even suspected they weren't cats at all but opossums, he was sure he'd caught some of them sleeping head down with their tails coiled round a branch, and the proof was their easy cohabitation – their complicity – with the birds in the tree), Lancelot tilted his head, tried to stay as still as possible, attempting to reduce his breathing to a minimum, keeping his balance by holding the window latch, as he watched his camphor tree and the cats who thought they were opossums.

He studied the sun's rays earnestly as they filtered

through the tree that quivered in the breeze. Shadows wavered delicately around him. Having watched the camphor tree for a long time, Lancelot went back to his proofreading and set to work again with a degree of delectation, rather like the brimming contentment he had felt as a child when his mother was cooking supper in the next room. (That is exactly what he thought when he tried to pinpoint the feeling – and Lancelot was a man who liked his precision. It reminds me of when I was a child, he thought to himself, when Mum was making supper and I could hear the radio burbling something inaudible, I felt good, as good as I do now…) Then he would smile and savour the physical pleasure, sitting back in his chair for a moment and smiling, almost succeeding in forgetting that his wife Elisabeth would soon be back talking to him as if he were a five-year-old.

It was when he met Irina that he realized what a gaping hole his life was.

THREE

One day Elisabeth went on a school trip with her pupils.

They all bundled into a coach and went off camping, equipped with porous tents and complicated neckerchiefs – his wife had made them herself on several successive evenings. Pedalling away on her sewing machine in the living room, she would lay out the pieces of fabric and select them according to some colour code Lancelot did not fully understand; in fact, at the time, he was watching programmes about big cats or the last dinosaurs, which did nothing to improve his understanding of his wife's huge undertaking, he could vaguely hear her explaining (to him?) how she had established the choice of fabrics and patterns (he was the only other person in the room) and how this selection process would make it so much easier for supervisors to save and identify a child if one of them should happen to tumble down a crevasse and call for help, desperately waving his or her brightly coloured scarf with an outstretched arm. Lancelot nodded as he witnessed the total disappearance of the last Mexican diplodocus population under a stream of meteorites, using the rest of his brain to think about the recipe for tuna simmered with soya and sugar that he was planning to concoct for himself the next day, but also to hurtle giddyingly away from his living room and find himself back in happy periods of his childhood spent with his pretty cousin Mimi, who came from a decadent branch of his family, read adult cartoons and initiated him into the diverse charms of their bodies. He concluded his reflections with the thought that there were certainly more edifying activities for young children than yomping through the mountains with a slightly deranged schoolmistress. Every now and then he glanced at his wife, thinking to himself, This woman is my wife, letting the sentence make sense in his mind, sighing imperceptibly and wondering exactly when everything had gone off the rails.

She left two days later, and Lancelot wandered about the empty apartment with great delight at first, then a touch of anxiety.

To fill his sudden redundancy, he started watching the furniture that occupied his life. He went from room to room with some satisfaction, not touching anything, looking at each item as if discovering it for the first time, studying things one after the other and cataloguing them: the ones he really cared about (what to do in the event of armed conflict? Leave them there or try to save some of them?);

those that seemed less indispensable; and those that had Swedish names. Stalking about with arms crossed, Lancelot established his hit parade of furniture. There was the Noguchi table which filled him with joy, the Charlotte Perriand bookshelves, and the armchair that was the spitting image of one which still had pride of place in the Villa Savoye. A whole lifetime spent choosing, buying, arranging and maintaining his tomb.

When Lancelot thought back to that day, he always tried to remember whether there was anything particular about the way the morning began, whether a sign might have alerted him to the fact that this day would turn his life upside down, whether there was something different about the light, whether the same old things were going on in the camphor tree in the courtyard, whether the world was going the usual way round.

It was the day he met Irina.

It seemed incredible to him, with hindsight, that that day could have started like any old weekday.

He had settled down to work and finished proofreading at about eleven o'clock, then he rang the editor he was working for to let him know.

Hello it's Lancelot.

Ah how are you Lancelot?

Yes... um... I've finished my proofreading... (He wondered why he always accompanied his telephone calls to this editor with little noises in his mouth – perhaps the man

made him feel uncomfortable, the embarrassment sometimes made him produce the odd absurd joke, which only
proved to the fellow at the other end that a proofreader's
choice of lifestyle – I live I eat I sleep I wank I work from
home, so send me a courier – was the sort of choice a
sociopath would make.)

Well you'd better start dancing then, replied the editor
who was himself experimenting with a still virginal form of
humour.

What?

No no nothing Lancelot… it was just a joke… I just
meant I haven't got anything else to offer you till Monday, I
can send a courier and…

No, Lancelot said, glancing at the camphor tree, one
buttock parked on the chest of drawers where his telephone
lived. I think I'm going to go out… I'll bring the proofs to
you…

Ah? A little walk round town? the editor said with some
surprise and to appear friendly, but his comment reinforced
Lancelot's conviction that the other man thought of him as
an outcast.

Yes. No.

Suit yourself.

See you later.

Lancelot hung up and stood there quite lost in the
enchantment he felt at the sight of his camphor tree (he
managed to spot a pair of albino blackbirds). He went over

to the window, nodded, opened both sides of the window and listened to the sound of the dozing tree, then tore himself away from his daydreaming, picked up a used brown envelope, carefully scribbled out the name of the previous addressee (himself), put on his sweater and went out.

Just as he was going outside something in the hallway caught his attention.

I'm sure, he thought to himself, there used to be a wardrobe here.

He stood there for a moment, perplexed.

If the wardrobe had disappeared, had everything inside it disappeared too?

Lancelot pulled a doubtful face for his own benefit, gave the beginnings of a nod as if to greet the absent wardrobe, and left with a slam of the door. He was not surprised that a wardrobe should disappear. Lancelot's world was a precarious, shifting place, and things appeared and disappeared according to a logic he could not grasp but readily accepted. Lancelot liked things going missing. It was a gentle reminder of parallel existences.

He went out into the snowscape of cherry blossom (tiny white discs scattered all over the ground), and it was such a deliciously lovely day that he decided to walk all the way to the publishing company. It might take him an hour but he couldn't see what else he was going to do with the vacant time he had on his hands before his next job, other than filling it watching cats jumping from branch to branch, reading a detective story (something classic, most likely an Agatha Christie) and drinking green tea. Lancelot did not cultivate any form of social life, because that would have made him feel he was dissipating his attention, it would have been like sowing little pebbles of concern, friendship and free time, which struck him as neither honest nor desirable. Lancelot maintained a pleasant solitude – the way other people devoted themselves to a sport or nurtured their bonsais – merely punctuated by his wife's lessons about things.

He walked for some time and went past a florist shop whose sign in stylized script with extravagant arabesques announced: *Once upon a rose...* (the ellipsis was all part of the name). He stopped to contemplate the nearest bouquets waiting patiently in their transparent pouches of water. The saleswoman leapt outside, and Lancelot gave her a not-buying shake of the head and set off again at a steady pace, but was stopped dead in his tracks by something which fell out of the sky and landed on his head, something which must have been, let's say, twenty-five centimetres by ten, and with a very smooth texture, which suggested to Lancelot the velvet of bed-hangings or what is commonly known as reverse leather, not that that has ever meant much to Lancelot because it seemed to him to refer to the inside of leather, and how can anyone believe the inside of an animal's skin is as soft as velvet? So Lancelot was hit on the head by

AND MY SEE-THROUGH HEART

an average-sized smooth object boasting a ten-centimetre heel totally sheathed in metal.

The heel cut his scalp slightly.

Lancelot gave a yelp of surprise and pain, he wanted to look up but was momentarily dazed, there was a sort of flash of light in the left-hand corner of his left eye which persuaded him he would be better off bending down and picking up the thing (a very elegant, size 4 woman's shoe) which had landed unceremoniously in the gutter. He looked at it carefully and thought to himself, What a perfect thing. And just as he was thinking this he heard a scream overhead.

He looked up in the hope of seeing the person who usually wore this shoe and that this person – he was surprised to find himself hoping this – would measure up to its perfection.

All he could see was an open window on the second floor of the building and, unless the shoe had tumbled straight out of the sky, which, when all was said and done, was too bold a hypothesis, there was a good chance it had come out of that window.

Lancelot hesitated, wavered for a moment, looking up at the window, then headed resolutely towards the front door of the building, which stood ajar. This was no mean feat for a man like Lancelot, who, many years previously, had made a vow of passivity. His creed of inertia had often put him at the mercy of tyranny and dependence, but had afforded him a pleasant and gradual decline – which was priceless to Lancelot. It was a nice way of living very slightly removed from actual events. Appearing to others as a peaceful sort of absence.

And in spite of the soothing detachment from the world that Lancelot cultivated, despite the wilful immobility of his vegetative life, he opened the door without further thought for what he was doing.

He went into a paved inner courtyard, prettified with large pots of sad, stupidly pink hydrangeas; went up the staircase that seemed most appropriate to reach the floor of the aforementioned window (an incredible staircase, with stone steps so worn they had become concave and leant oddly towards the banisters, so that the best way of climbing them seemed to be to hug the wall and keep a watchful eye on the shuddering that ran through the banisters as you drew near to a landing). Lancelot thought to himself, I may not be able to leave this place, and eventually arrived on the second floor. He knocked on the relevant door (and heard a lot of commotion inside), waited a moment, knocked again, leant over to read the name on the label on the door, Irina something, and just as he was leaning over, still in that unfavourable position (neck thrust forward, back arched), the door was flung open to reveal a woman who stared at him.

What? she yelled, as if he were a good deal more than fifteen centimetres away.

I came about the shoe, Lancelot managed, trying to recover what his mother called composure, waving the shoe in question in his right hand and keeping his left arm clamped by his side to protect his package of proofs from potential lightning bolts.

What shoe?

It fell on the pavement. (Lancelot suddenly felt very weary, confronted with this far from affable creature.) On my head first, then the pavement.

So?

I thought it came from your window.

The young woman looked at him, looked at the shoe, and then seemed to understand what he was on about. She spun on her heel and shrieked into the apartment beyond her, Fuckwit number one, I've got Fuckwit number two here (Lancelot swallowed hard) and he's been hit on the head by your slut's shoe. You wouldn't be chucking them out of the window to get rid of them so I don't find them, would you?

Lancelot thought, It's high time I made my exit.

A man much older than her popped his head round one of the doors that gave onto the hall. Lancelot thought, I really do need to make my exit. The man looked at them. Do you know him? he asked the young woman. Lancelot felt more and more tired, if anyone had asked him how old he was he would have said, A hundred and two. He thought about how his day had started, thought about the cherry blossom scattered on the ground, sighed and said, I'll be going, then threw the shoe to the man, who shot out an arm to catch it mid flight. Have your property back, Lancelot enunciated, with what he hoped was a degree of panache, and he turned away. He went down the stairs using the same cautious technique as on the way up, walked past the desperate hydrangeas in the courtyard and went back out into the quiet of the street, only then realizing how much the chill of the old stones in that building had felt like a tomb. Lancelot shuddered, muttered, Now where was I? trying, with this, to rekindle his pleasant disposition from before the unfortunate incident, sniffing the air around him, closing his eyes for a second to concentrate and stifle the occasional wave of anxiety which caught up with him right there in the street (and was related to an amorphous feeling of unease which projected him straight back to his childhood, I'm a quiet, serious little boy who's misunderstood and nostalgic before his time). He still held the package of proofs tightly to him, trying to get back into his peaceful mood, as if it were made up of molecules slowly dispersing in the breeze and breaking him completely apart, breathing steadily (The danger, Mr Rubinstein, is that you'll hyperventilate, if you start breathing too hard and too fast, then, bang, you're overwhelmed by anxiety) and trying to recover some of his serenity.

Lancelot calmed down and, just as he was setting off again, the front door opened behind him and the disagreeable creature from the second floor flew out onto the pavement, still scrambling into her clothes, scanning the street for someone, and finding him – Lancelot – all useless there on the tarmac. She strode over to him with a belligerence that made him sigh inwardly. Oh no, he thought, without actually saying anything, but with such a desolate expression on his face that the woman from the second floor effected an imperceptible pause as she studied his face. When she was close enough, she ventured:

I wanted to apologize...

Oh it's nothing, Lancelot interrupted her, out of a sort of habitual courtesy.

No it's not nothing.

And she looked at him and he saw her for the first time, and what he saw made him groan inwardly, It should have been such a quiet day, he said to himself, and what he saw was a young woman with unusual eyes, olive skin and black hair that coiled and swung as if it had a life of its own, the arch of her eyebrows so moved Lancelot that he almost cried, She's a darling, a treasure, he told himself, then he glanced at her feet to check whether, to cap it all, she was wearing one of those perfect pairs of shoes, and she was wearing a perfect pair of shoes (dark red with a tiny golden buckle on one side, and narrow grey heels) and he almost moaned. She had thrown on a beige raincoat (Lancelot's mother always used to say, A putty-colour mac), and there was nothing more to this girl (she was no longer a woman at all) than her face and her ideal shoes, and that was enough for Lancelot to fall in love, and Lancelot silently despaired, he was overwhelmed by a terrible weariness, he looked upwards to try to calm himself and saw the trees along the avenue and their rustling foliage, he sighed and heard her ask:

Can I walk with you for a couple of minutes?

So, without another word, he continued on his way and she set off in step with him. That's what Lancelot thought to himself, She's in step with me, the expression pleased him and he thought it very weird to be walking side by side with this girl and her perfect shoes, and he told himself, Everyone can see us, which must have meant, Everyone envies me, and when he felt that surge of miserable pride wash over him, he begged himself to unwind again, Lancelot Lancelot Lancelot, he said, Don't go getting ideas, and on they walked together, with him gradually slowing his footsteps so that he matched the girl's pace.

FOUR

But Elisabeth came back. She turned up in the apartment with her rucksack, her rolled-up sleeping mat, her walking boots and her pink nose, and Lancelot stood up from his desk to greet her. Or perhaps it was to watch her twirling about, as he would have done with some rare species of Coleoptera.

The minute she set foot in the apartment she started talking – although Lancelot suspected she never stopped and he merely caught snatches of an endless stream of speech when he came near her. He tilted his head to one side and thought, This can't go on. This thought was, of course, driven by his recent meeting with Irina (three days ago), a meeting that had turned him so completely upside down that it would now be impossible to pick up his life where he had left it. He surprised himself by coming straight out and saying:

The wardrobe's disappeared (a comment accompanied by a raising of his eyebrows and shoulders, which meant a combination of, It's not important, it's nothing to do with me and I couldn't give a damn).

She did not respond to this but just stood there with all her gear at her feet. She had long arms, much longer than average and this, in days gone by, had lent her movements a peculiar sort of grace, like an Indian dancer, but at this precise moment, because she was standing slightly hunched, having dumped her kit on the floor, it made her look like a depressive hag.

It's been Bermuda Triangled, Lancelot went on with a smile. He had found the expression in a book, it had amused him, now he was claiming it as his own, but apparently, judging by the look his wife shot him, it was not producing the expected effect – mind you, he hadn't been aspiring to a peal of laughter, he would just have appreciated a knowing nod of the head, but the only complicity she offered was to look at him wide-eyed.

This whole scene reinforced the notion that he needed to get out of there as soon as possible.

He thought to himself, My Irina, my princess, my brand new treasure is waiting for me on the other side of town. I'm so desperate to see her again it hurts (and he did actually feel sharp little pains in every extremity of his body, as if he were being pricked by dozens of sea urchins).

Simultaneous relationships make for unfairness. Lancelot was just looking for signs to confirm his decision and, whatever his wife Elisabeth's attitude, that decision existed without her – and everything she said and even the way she stood distanced him from her and made him a little more determined.

What are you talking about? she said.

Then she went back to her monologue while she put her things away in the bedroom and went into the kitchen to drink some fruit juice, with Lancelot following her, watching her every move, as if to engrave them on his memory, so he would always remember the way she opened the fridge and closed it with a flick of her elbow, how she studiously left everything very clean. Elisabeth washed her glass as soon as she had finished using it and carried on with her indefatigable account of her travels with her pupils, clearly paying very little attention to the fact that Lancelot was not listening, turning round on herself and wittering away so that Lancelot failed to hear a single one of her sentences from beginning to end.

It was when she was in their bedroom unpacking her clothes onto the bed (the sight of their communal bed suddenly made Lancelot want to heave, and the thought of spending another night with her to the left of him seemed unimaginable) that he said:

I'm going to leave, Irina.

And what he meant to say had become grotesque because of confusing the names. Meanwhile Elisabeth looked up and said:

I'm not called Irina.

Lancelot tried everything he could to reverse the march of time and destroy that momentary slip, to try to restore some semblance of dignity and not give the name of his new beloved to the woman he was leaving. He stammered, she hesitated. She could have saved face for him by agreeing to believe he had got muddled with the name of a character in the book he was proofreading, but she didn't – why would she? – and simply replied:

You've hardly got any stuff to take from here anyway.

She made a sweeping gesture with her arms which precluded any claim on Lancelot's part to the Noguchi table and the Charlotte Perriand bookcase.

We'll treat all this as spoils of war, she announced.

She looked him right in the eye and he felt as he used to feel being with this woman with her long white arms. He could find nothing to add and managed to say, OK OK, as if she were the one imposing a decision on him. He turned away and walked along the corridor to the living room to pick up his new bundle of proofs which he had not yet corrected (because of all the upheaval obviously), and noticed that the grandfather clock had disappeared too, and he felt that the further he walked towards the apartment door the more the things he had known faded before his eyes, it was as if he now needed to run to avoid disappearing along with them, he quickened his pace, the chest of drawers was growing hazy and started flickering over to his right, the umbrella stand had left not a single trace, Lancelot started running to reach the door, he opened it and closed it behind him, trying not to slam it too hard, because there was no reason why he should slam it, Elisabeth was not angry or trying to hang on to him by the tails of his white shirt. He came to a standstill now, quite sure that everything behind the door had been swallowed up. He listened, could hear nothing at first, then detected something like the moaning or sobbing of a small animal – it reminded him of the feeble squeaks of a trapped mouse. He took a few steps back and stood for a while facing that wooden door with its double lock. It seemed so familiar. And it was like leaving Ithaca with the knowledge he would never return. Lancelot sighed and thought to himself, I don't know how to leave women, as if he had been in the habit of making a dignified bow, when in fact he only ever regretted his own shyness and awkwardness, his experience in matters of break-ups being pitifully limited.

Lancelot went down the stairs into the courtyard where the camphor tree still housed every opossum-cat in the neighbourhood. He spared no time to stop under the tree but went through the porch and out onto the street feeling light and free – all he had left was his bundle of proofs, his espadrilles and his white shirt, darned at the elbow (by Elisabeth).

He set off towards Irina's house.

FIVE

On the way to Irina's apartment Lancelot thought about his wife. You should never compare your wife with your mistress. The wife wins every time. His mother had always told him (and she knew a thing or two about this, given that all through Lancelot's childhood she had more than her fair share of walking out and being walking out on) that a man takes a mistress to stay with his wife while a wife takes a lover to leave her husband (she had waited four years for her lover, a husband and father, to leave home, but he ended up moving to Majorca with his two sons and newly pregnant wife).

And Lancelot wondered, Is it my feminine side?

He walked on and his footsteps set up their own rhythm saying, I left my wife today.

He cut across avenues and still his footsteps said, I left my wife today.

And all at once he remembered how they had first met. The memory struck him brutally like a blow to the head. He had not thought about it for years, but in the early days of their relationship he used to fan the flames by thinking back to how they met.

He had fallen in love with the nape of Elisabeth's neck and her long white arms. He watched them at the university library. It felt like seeing someone moving underwater. Elisabeth had the slow, harmonious movements of a person travelling through a medium with a different consistency and density from the substance common mortals exist in. He was slightly in awe of Elisabeth right up to the day he spoke to her as she was coming out of the library, when she proved chatty and friendly. He approached her on the steps, asking a stupid, pompous question (he was studying history of art) about what was beautiful and what was not. She stopped and answered by saying she didn't have an answer, but that, even though she didn't understand it, she herself adhered to the concept that an artist's shit in a box was more of a work of art than a painting of a landscape with a windmill covered in wisteria and two fawns frolicking in the meadow in the background.

They were young and inexperienced.

Lancelot looked at her and long after that he would remember her high-collared white broderie anglaise dress (worn ironically), the glitter of her fake ruby earrings, and her calm pale eyes. He decided there and then that he would marry her and she would be the mother of his children.

Nineteen years later Lancelot was walking out on her.

Leaving her in an apartment where things were disappearing, and saying the wrong name on his way out.

Lancelot grimaced and started walking gingerly, as if the soles of his feet were burnt. He felt sad. There seemed to be a little voice in his head taking pleasure in sending him nostalgic thoughts just when he had decided to change his life, a voice whispering there was still time to turn back and make amends, he could always go back to the gently flowing if sparsely populated waters of his existence.

Lancelot saw some children playing war games on the pavement next to a stretch of wasteland where some brick buildings had been knocked down to make way for what would be a retirement home. There were three children, one was carrying a plastic gun which looked so real that only the ease with which he handled it gave away that it was a toy, the other two were running after him shouting, We're going to rape you and slit your throat, so Lancelot stopped and watched them climb over the fence with its NO ENTRY sign, then saw them drop their guns and assume karate poses, issuing what they thought were the appropriate noises (the noise boys make when they imitate a speeding car). He parked himself next to the barrier and thought, I'm very glad I don't have any children, even though broadly speaking that was not true, but it was now, now that he was leaving Elisabeth, and having children with her would have complicated things considerably. Lancelot set off again and almost bumped into a woman wearing such huge glasses they reminded him of a diving mask and he half expected her to be carrying a harpoon; next he came across a young woman with a little girl, the girl was holding the woman's hand and the latter was wearing a very short skirt and very high heels, the child had her tiny face turned up towards the young woman, who was most likely her mother, and was saying, And in my dream the nasty man took my key, but I put it inside something really strong and magical and full of jewels. Lancelot walked on past them and heard the child say, Are you listening? and even now that he was a really long way from the woman and her little girl, he could still hear her saying, Are you listening, are you listening, are you listening? And Lancelot thought she might invent her dreams to get her mother to listen to her.

Eventually he found himself outside Irina's building, by the florist and its ready-made bouquets. He looked up at his beloved's window, it was closed, and he thought, Maybe she's not there. The little voice whispered, Maybe she's left for good, she's packed her bags and is standing in the bistro over the road laughing to herself while she knocks back a glass of strong neat spirit and sniggers at your naivety. Lancelot managed not to turn round to check whether there actually was a bistro and whether Irina was lying in ambush there. He took a deep breath and opened the heavy front door of the building, then went up the murderous staircase and knocked on Irina's door. He heard the click-clack of her footsteps on the wooden floor. And sighed with gratitude,

Thank you thank you thank you. Irina opened the door wide and stood on the threshold, quite motionless, so that – you might think – Lancelot had all the time in the world to look at her. She was wearing four articles of clothing which made Lancelot's heart and his dick leap. A black vinyl corset that gleamed in the half light, black satin gloves that came up to her elbows, a pair of shiny hot pants and twelve-centimetre heels (the shoes looked purple but there was too little light to be sure). Lancelot swallowed hard and thought, If I hadn't come along would she have stayed here waiting in that outfit? And the fact that she had accepted the possible humiliation of disappointment (pacing up and down her empty apartment in black vinyl or sprawling on the sofa in all that pointless paraphernalia with the little creaking noise her every move would have made, each creak reminding her of her torment), the risk of that humiliation made her both magnificent and touching. Lancelot smiled at her and that was when a new voice which would not leave him for years to come popped up in his mind and breathed, Come on, Lancelot, you should be asking yourself who gave her all that gear, or worse, dear friend, because there is something worse, who was she trying to please, before you, when she bought such a daft get-up?

SIX

Lancelot had heard the telephone ring.

He opened an eye. He was not at home, in the bedroom he shared with Elisabeth. He felt giddily disorientated because he didn't immediately recognize this bed. He sat up and looked around.

What the hell am I doing here?

Funerals! Irina cursed in the corridor.

The memories came back. He dropped down onto the pillow.

He stared up at the ceiling, the mouldings and the pipework snaking along the walls. There was something decrepit and snug about the room which produced an inappropriate languor in him. On the desk next to a window a wilting bouquet of irises looked ready to fall apart. Above them, dominating the room, was a mirror set in an elaborate plaster moulding full of garlands and climbing plants – whatever sort of concupiscent scenes had it reflected before now? Lancelot wondered. A cluttered, gravity-defying bookcase. Clothes strewn about like hillocks of different colours. An old family chest of drawers, full to the brim and squat on its feet.

Carrot-top had her babies behind the chest of drawers, Lancelot's mother always used to sing.

What was that song? Was it being nasty? Was it racist? His mother would have denied that, Of course not, of course it isn't, it's about a ginger cat having her kittens...

What the hell am I doing here?

Piles of books and pairs of shoes, all with such high heels that they readily existed without the feet that wore them – flat moccasins always look abandoned, incomplete and pitiful, but shoes with spiky heels live their fairytale lives without anyone's support, even lying about on the floor, on dodgy old lino, they still have miraculous grace and distant splendour.

Lancelot so loved women in high heels.

Oh yes of course.

Carrot-top had her babies behind the chest of drawers.

High-heeled shoes.

Late afternoon light from behind the closed curtains hung hazily in the room.

Have I been asleep in the middle of the afternoon?

He heard Irina whispering in the corridor (so as not to wake you, wouldn't you say?), heard her stifled exclamations, using her peculiar swear word again, then going on murmuring.

She hung up.

Carrot-top had her babies behind the chest of drawers.

The footsteps were coming closer, she nudged the bedroom door open with her shoulder, then appeared – and now Lancelot could no longer ask what he was doing there; all was clear again. She smiled, Are you awake? and put a tray down on the desk. On it she had put a teapot, a cup, a glass and a bottle of cheap gin.

Lancelot thought, uh-oh, would my beloved be a drinker?

She poured a cup of tea and handed it to him, he took it, brought it to his lips, and burnt his tongue and the roof of his mouth, but carried on scalding himself so as not to lose face.

She drank her gin as she watched him, sitting on the edge of the bed wrapped in a white dressing gown in waffled cotton (another reminder of his mother, who knew every kind of fabric by name) and with a golden insignia on the chest.

Did you steal that from a hotel? Lancelot asked, indicating the robe.

Irina smiled, didn't answer and turned towards the window. A nonchalant silence settled between them. A comfortable feeling which still managed to arouse subtle anxiety in Lancelot. Urging him to carry on scalding himself with some determination. And stare at Irina's face. Then look away to avoid burdening this woman with all his expectations so soon.

He tried to put off the moment of telling her he had absolutely no intention of going home to his wife, that he didn't have any belongings there he minded about (not the books he had already read nor the beige trousers and matching polo shirts he had worn in his former life), that he could come and live with her this very minute and put the nineteen years he had spent with his wife behind him. He suspected that the suggestion of his immediate installation in Irina's life might not delight her.

He tried to remember whether he had read or seen or heard tell of a situation like this and whether there was, therefore, some way in which he could just do a twirl and announce point blank – but with humour and a lightness of touch – that she was the love of his life. He could not think of anything. It felt as if his neurons were struggling in gelatine. And all they wanted was to be allowed to quench themselves in contemplating Irina's face.

Lancelot sighed and, without help from his neurons or his reading, felt like saying he thought something special was going on between them. Something unusual. Luckily, she did not give him the chance.

I'm off to Slovenia in two days' time, she announced.

She paused for a moment while she tied up her hair.

I'm going to film bears.

A hole opened up under Lancelot, there was a chasm under the bed, he was sucked into the abyss, where he could scream and fight as much as he liked, he clung to the sheets and tensed. He managed a smile but it looked nothing like one. To film bears? he said, and she nodded and said very gently:

Yes, do you remember, it's my job.

Your job's filming bears? (He could hear the shrill querulous note in his own voice.)

No, it's filming animals in general.

Ah ha.

The DP called because the last director encountered some difficulties...

What sort of difficulties? Lancelot managed (while internally it came out as: but what's a DP?).

The bear came across him one night and the guy got eaten.

Eaten eaten?

Eaten eaten.

Really?

The bear ate what he could and buried the rest. For later, she explained.

And you're off to take this guy's place?

Actually (flick of her right hand which sweeps open the stolen robe, revealing a portion of her vinyl corset, an utterly incongruous intrusion at this point), I don't think he was very careful... I've worked with him before... (And here Lancelot, king of the misplaced thought, wondered, Has she slept with him before too?) He was the sort who didn't follow any of the basic safety regulations...

VÉRONIQUE OVALDÉ

Lancelot had the unpleasant feeling she was reciting lines, he frowned, felt slightly sick.

Paul? she said.

Lancelot looked up with a start.

I haven't got a good feeling about this, he moaned.

I have.

I meant the bears.

So did I.

Will you be there long?

Not very. A few weeks.

A few? (He hated himself for going on about this but there was no other way he could do it.)

Three. I think.

I'll wait for you, he said. And he nodded his head as if he were the one granting her this time, and as if he had perfectly mastered the situation and the leaping jig of his heart. He took her hand and drew her closer.

I'll wait for you...

he thought, My treasure my beloved my sunshine,

You'll come back safe and sound...

he took her in his arms,

I'll wait for you... he said again,

and just as he took her terribly gently in his arms, stroking her hair and her face, making out her sparrow's bones, just as he did, Lancelot felt he could forget the stolen robe, the creaking vinyl and man-eating bears.

38

SEVEN

When he had walked beside Irina the first time, the day she wore her awful putty-coloured mac, with her hair breaking away from its chignon in wild wisps (which had an aquatic quality, like black seaweed wafting limply), her silhouette tiny beside him despite the teetering grey heels, the bags beneath her Byzantine mosaic eyes forming great blue arcs, every part of her glowing in such a distinctive way – that was what Lancelot had thought to himself, he could not express it in any other terms – when he had walked beside Irina the first time, he was so bowled over he finally had a glimpse of his life properly in proportion.

When she had taken him back to her apartment after having a first cup of coffee together outside, when she had opened the door announcing that she'd broken up once and for all with the lowlife who spent his time in her apartment inviting girls up and drinking her gin, that it had been brewing for a long time, and that there hadn't been anything between them for a while anyway, that the business with the

shoe chucked out of the window had been the last straw,
that he would never set foot back in her place, and actually
she was going to call the locksmith right now to change all
the locks (she'd taken his keys but, she said, he might just be
twisted enough to have made another set and gone on using
Irina's apartment as his bachelor pad), when she had offered
Lancelot another cup of coffee with her, when she had told
him she liked being with him on that gloomy day, when she
had decreed that Lancelot really was an impossible name
and that he'd have to have something more modest, like Paul
for example – Paul's good and short, it's effective, if
someone calls it in the street, you turn round, it's perfect in
emergencies, that sort of name – when she had taken off her
putty-coloured mac, when he had wondered, How old can
she be? when he had looked around and seen a hotchpotch
of photos on the walls (giraffes, children, Bosnian villages,
house fires, seaside views, phosphorescent jellyfish), when
he had looked around the room to avoid looking at her too
much, when he had stayed standing while she made him an
espresso and when he had stood facing each wall as if at a
museum, when she had positioned herself close to him,
touched his arm, then his hand, when she had put her fist in
the palm of Lancelot's hand, had kissed him and led him to
the bedroom, when she had drawn the curtains and when he
had lain her down and undressed her (and he had thought,
But Lancelot, I thought you were so faint-hearted!), when he
had fucked her and she'd said, You're hurting me, Paul, and

he had apologized (thinking, I don't even recognize you, Lancelot, where's the faint heart now?), when he had rested his head on his beauty's breast, sinking momentarily into a state of confusion, wondering what he was doing there, given that he no longer remembered desire, given that he'd made do without sexuality for years (as had Elisabeth), thinking, I'm in such a state, already worrying then refusing to worry, then muddling everything up, wondering, What's happened to make me end up here, in this bed, with this pretty girl? and the next question which was just as disturbing, What on earth can she see in someone like me? and another one, Is it really normal to go from one disastrous choice to another within a matter of hours, and what does that haste mean? and also, Am I dealing with a nymphomaniac? Lancelot kissing her skin which was fine and un-perfumed, Lancelot, grateful and moved, thinking, I'm not going to cry, though... so when he had gone through all this, had finally put his arms round her and kissed her eyelids, Lancelot knew there could be no other solution than to stay by her side if he wanted to carry on feeling alive.

EIGHT

Irina went off to film her bears. And Lancelot moved into her apartment.

She rang him from a call box when she went to the village for provisions. She spoke to him tenderly and told him about what she was filming, her encounters with bears, her waiting and her nights spent under canvas.

Lancelot could sit for hours next to the telephone, resting his head on a cushion so he could fall asleep when the fancy took him, the cushion laid flat on the table, and him sitting facing the table, his arms dropping to the floor when he went to sleep, waking when the contraption started ringing in his ears, not picking up till Irina's first word on the answering machine, his heart beating, and at the end of the call, frustrated, only able to tell her how happy he was to hear her, the conversation never satisfying his expectations, it was just Irina's voice transcribed into electric impulses giving him news of her, talking about the two men she was working with, giving him details of technical incidents, when what Lancelot wanted was extravagances and promises of eternal love, and – even though she was affectionate on the telephone – uncertainties wormed their way into Lancelot's mind, he asked himself, Is she really in Slovenia (yes, she was there, or she had a thing for complicated scenarios because he had received two postcards posted in Ljubljana, signed by her), he asked himself, Who did she actually go with? He told himself, She thinks she cares for me because she's lost in the middle of the mountains but when she gets home she'll realize she feels nothing of the sort, he told himself, She only reassures me on the phone because she's kind.

In between his pernicious thoughts Lancelot had a little nap, his head on Irina's table.

After a couple of days of this routine he pulled himself together and went out in the afternoons to sit on the bench in the courtyard with the hydrangeas, and read detective novels, he cooked himself pasta with spicy sauce, listened to Bach on Irina's machine, opened the shutters and watered the plants. He looked after the apartment like the perfect caretaker. He concocted a pretty cosmetic little world for when she came home. He forced himself to resist opening her letters or holding them up to the light to peer at them, goaded as he occasionally was by his own domestic demon, he arranged her letters in categories, he left the windows open all day and became increasingly serene as he answered Irina's successive telephone calls, even managing to be surprised they were so regular, speaking steadily to her and being as sincere as possible in taking an interest in her life with the bears.

He succeeded in not worrying if he had no news of her for several days. At first he pictured her torn limb from limb by the claws of a crazed grizzly, now he kept his calm and told himself, Either way she'll call me as soon as she can, or if something has happened to her someone would have let me know (he had made her promise she would carry a card saying he should be contacted in the event of a mishap).

It was a strange situation, having spent only a few days with this woman, having overturned the life he had led up until then and being here now waiting for her. He liked it when the concierge came and gave him the mail, he opened the door to her and smiled at her gratefully as if her involvement legitimized Lancelot's presence in the apartment. He ended up offering her a coffee, and she sat down in Irina's shambolic kitchen, puffing and sweating. She announced that her name was Vladimir, that she was a transsexual, that her breasts were sprouting and that it was the craziest and most disappointing experience she had had in her life.

Disappointing? said Lancelot.

And Vladimir sat there with her coffee and cognac, and explained that she still felt just as lonely, that she knew all the hormones she was taking would eventually give her cancer, and that her children still didn't want to see her.

Lancelot did not know what to say.

He took Vladimir's flaccid hand in his own and patted it, he offered her some more cognac and told her he had just left his wife, had no children and virtually nothing in his bank account, and was worried that the woman he loved was going to be eaten by a bear.

Vladimir took Lancelot's head, brought it to rest on her brand new bosom, holding it there with her two great paws, and started to sob. Lancelot stayed there, leaning forwards, with Vladimir's hand on the back of his neck, listening out for Vladimir's heartbeats in between her jolting sobs. He tried to get back up once but Vladimir's fist would not let go, so Lancelot gave in to Vladimir's despair, there in Irina's kitchen, sitting on a sky-blue Formica chair. He felt Vladimir was crying for the two of them, for their Terrible Misfortune. And he found the thought comforting.

Vladimir reappeared regularly for sessions like this.

After her visits, Lancelot sat in an armchair by an open window and listened to sounds out on the avenue, or he went down and parked himself on the hydrangea bench and did the thing that, when all was said and done, he was best at:

He waited for Irina.

Irina came back.

Lancelot called a solicitor and began divorce proceedings. He only saw Elisabeth again on the day of the hearing. He did not use the opportunity to try to speak to her or explain himself further. She bundled together any administrative documents that concerned him personally, sent them to his employer's address and did not make contact with him again.

Lancelot often thought of her.

Just before moving to Catano with Irina, he took to spending every day outside the school where Elisabeth taught. You could see the playground from the street. He would stand there, leaning against a plane tree, looking at little girls in uniform skipping about on the tarmac, watching his tall and beautiful ex-wife in her homemade clothes walking up and down the playground with the slow regularity of a Platonic philosopher. Lancelot tilted his head, resting his shoulder against the smooth two-tone bark, he crossed his arms over his chest and then went back to be with Irina.

PART TWO

NINE

There is a car in the Omoko river, one Lancelot does not recognize.

It is dark, an icy black dark that pierces the sinuses with every breath, but the police have set up massively powerful projectors to light up the river. The place is crawling with people in the darkness. Lancelot thinks, Funny to have all these people for one car in the water. He has got out of his own, and is now coming over very slowly, feeling as if his body is going alternately limp and stiff, which means he cannot walk normally. People try to stop him but he says, I'm the victim's husband, and adds, I think, for his own benefit, not really sure whether he thinks he is her husband or thinks she is the victim. Flashing lights blink all round him and everything happens in peculiar silence. He would have imagined a situation like this being dominated by a tremendous hubbub, an agitated intensity of sound, unless all of a sudden, as he walks towards the bank, he has gone deaf.

Snow falls conscientiously over the scene. It is so fresh it makes Lancelot feel that with every footstep he is crushing minute invertebrates which would rather stay silent and be pulverized than raise their voices against him.

Someone pulls him by the sleeve and says, Detective Schneider's expecting you, and Lancelot sees the ambulance and thinks, If there's an ambulance then she can't be dead, and he adds, God be praised, surprising himself to be bringing God into all this, and realizing that resorting to the unexplained becomes inevitable in circumstances like these. A tall man appears and swivels him in the direction of Detective Schneider, who is turned away from them and appears to be a woman, judging by the pink parka. Detective, the man calls, and Detective Schneider turns round, she is busy with some assistant, and Lancelot says to himself, My God she's enormous, and he wonders, Doesn't the police force have physical training that's incompatible with obesity?

She comes over to him and shakes his hand, Are you Mr Rubinstein? The woman's hand is vigorous, and Lancelot notices how deep-set and mobile her eyes are, and thinks, All her organs are being compressed by fat; he would like to talk to her about it but understands that it is just his brains sending him parasitic messages so that he doesn't focus on what matters. He says, Where's my wife? and Detective Schneider gestures with her right hand, In there. Lancelot looks in the direction she is pointing, and sees the ambulance setting off. But where are they taking her? he asks. Detective Schneider turns to her assistant, who replies, Milena, then adds, I don't think you can go with her but we'll follow by car and you can sign the death certificate.

This is a bit too abrupt for Lancelot, he falls to his knees in the snow.

The fat woman cries out in surprise, leans forward, wanting to help him up, and yelps, Hasn't anyone told him? She seems both embarrassed and irritated. Lancelot has decided to disappear under the snow, he has started burying himself, taking great armfuls of snow and covering himself over with it, the fat woman bellows, Is someone going to come and help me? Lancelot is making a hole for himself in the snow and fights off anyone who tries to touch him, they form a circle round him, Lancelot is constructing his lair, working away in projector-lit silence, he wants to erase himself, diving deep into the thick layer of snow. One man comments, as if he knows about things, Dogs do this sometimes, no one replies, they all seem lost in their own thoughts, with the economy of movement typical of those who have already done more than their quota of overtime, then Detective Schneider snaps out of it and cries, Get him out of there and take him away.

They get Lancelot out and take him away.

And as they lead him off, Lancelot's head lolls and he feels the world crazing over and breaking like an eggshell.

TEN

Lancelot is making himself tea. He gazes into the distance through the kitchen window as he pours water into the kettle. You can see up to the road, the frozen trees glittering in the morning light like candy canes, and on the left a late fox running for cover in the woods, making great muddled leaps through the snow.

Lancelot feels very slightly detached from himself. It is as if he is not only filling the kettle but also standing right beside the sink watching himself do it. To be fair, he watches himself affectionately. He feels patient and duplicated.

It must be the medicine Doctor Epstein gave him producing this comfortable doubling process.

He can use this kettle without thinking about the fact that Irina bought it, he can park himself in front of the sink without instantly remembering that Irina fought to hang onto this awful stone sink, which is so low down you would have thought the previous occupants of the house were dwarves – if your height corresponds more or less to the norm then when you do the washing-up your thighs end up completely splattered.

Lancelot, thanks to Doctor Epstein's medicine, can manage not to think about Irina for a fraction of a second. The rest of the time it is as if his blood pulses with memories coated in shards of glass.

He lays his hands flat in the smooth stone basin, thinking that if he were a drinker then, even this early in the morning, he would have had a strong drink, a spirit, a vodka, stuff which smells of ageing aunts and the filigree of crochet over velvet armrests, Lancelot tells himself, There's nothing better for coping with grief, and with that the memory of his drowned Irina smacks him full in the face again. And, more particularly, the conversation he had at the beginning of the week with Detective Schneider, the one that gave him a Very Big Additional Shock.

And it is as he stands facing the window above the sink, letting the water overflow from the kettle, and he is also just to the side watching with interest as the streaming water splashes his trousers, that Lancelot sees a figure coming over to the house. He leans forwards, wipes the condensation from the pane and tries to recognize the person coming towards him across the snowy meadow. Definitely the law. Since Irina's death, they haven't stopped coming and asking him questions.

He watches the man come closer.

He says to himself, He's limping.

He says to himself, Is he ill?

He thinks about what Irina said before asking him (or rather demanding with that way she had of mimicking loopiness or a descent into depression if, by chance, anyone looked about to thwart her whim) whether they could leave Camerone. She argued that she could no longer bear seeing so many people in the streets, the underground or the bus, she couldn't help picturing their intestines throbbing inside them, she could see all that breathless red meat and those coloured liquids which served them as lives, it had become unbearable living alongside these skinned creatures the whole time.

Lancelot drives away this memory.

He heads for the front door to greet the man.

Hello, the latter says when Lancelot opens the door. He appears to be a little over sixty, long and thin like army officers in films, a man who might seem dangerous if he did not look so tired. His face has the concave shape of the starving. He is wearing a fur-lined jacket and heavy walking boots covered in snow. I left my car up there, he says, pointing to the road. Lancelot pops his head out of the doorway to see where the man is pointing, he cannot see a car but nods anyway. I'm not disturbing you, the man asks, but it does not sound like a question at all, he seems pretty sure that it would be impossible to disturb Lancelot early in the morning. Lancelot shrugs and says, I was making some tea. Then the man replies, Perfect, without even a smile, he takes a step into the house, holds out his hand and says (and he already has one foot inside the wretched house, and Lancelot looks at the snow-covered boot dripping on his doormat and feels he is losing track of things), the man says, I'm Irina's father. And Lancelot shakes his hand, screwing up his eyes and trying to remember what it is this man is meant to have died of, because Irina told him, he is sure she did, that her father was dead.

Lancelot finds something very familiar about this man's face, and he's immeasurably grateful to him for it. The fellow has the same eyes as Irina and it is a pleasure seeing them alive and moving again. He stands aside to let him in and says, Irina told me you were dead. The man stamps his clumpy boots on the mat in the doorway, then takes them off and stands there in his socks as he replies, That doesn't surprise me.

Lancelot shows him into the living room and beats a retreat to the kitchen, stops in front of the sink and clings to the edge of it, letting his gaze drift off through the window. His head is spinning pleasantly, Doctor Epstein's medicine affords him not only a degree of comfort but also a pasty sort of giddiness.

He waits for the kettle to start whistling, not strong enough to confront the upright old man in the living room unless his hands are occupied with a litre of scalding water.

When Lancelot goes back to join him, he is annoyed to see that the man has sat himself down in his favourite armchair with the fake zebra-skin cushions. He thinks of asking to change places, then resigns himself to sitting opposite him on the velvet sofa where Irina liked to read (in fact he is perfectly happy adopting the position she used to take when she read, the velvet is slightly worn, corresponding to strategic parts of her living body, her elbows, hips and ankles).

I heard the news from the paper, Irina's father announces.

. Lancelot lowers his eyelids as a sign of assent – he is busy deliberately burning the roof of his mouth, as he likes doing.

I haven't spoken to Irina's mother about it, the man goes on, she's a bit fragile. So I just set off, telling her I was going trout fishing in the north (he laughs at his ingenuity).

And didn't she probe any further? Lancelot enquires, not that he feels concerned about the secrets Irina's parents keep from each other but because he would now like some semblance of conversation.

She hasn't talked for a long time, the man replies steadily. She had a stroke some time ago now.

Lancelot nods, picturing an old mute version of Irina in a leaf-print armchair, glued to the television. Despair rears its head. He wonders, Why on earth didn't Irina want anything more to do with these people? He shakes his head, he would like to swallow a couple of miracle pills but has trouble making up his mind to do it in front of Irina's father. He asks himself, Have I got the strength to get up and find an excuse to disappear into the kitchen? He sighs, no, he hasn't got the heart at the moment.

The man is waiting for his tea to cool a little, he looks around as if thinking of buying the house.

Have you been here long? he asks. And Lancelot is thankful for his not putting every sentence in the past.

Nearly two years.

And before that?

We were in Camerone.

Ah (the man tests some of his tea, hastily withdraws the cup from his lips and goes on), last time I saw Irina she was living with a male nurse in Camerone, he used to hang posters and was a militant member of the Cric...

The Cric?

A really radical anti-vivisection movement. I don't even know if the letters of that acronym mean anything... (he seems to think about this then abandons the subject with a slightly contemptuous smirk).

I didn't know about that, says Lancelot.

Ooooh... She was very young at the time. Just a little girl.

Ah. And you haven't seen her since then?

I wanted to meet you (and this is like a declaration of friendship, it comes accompanied by a smile, the only one this man's face is capable of producing, a rather sad, grimacing thing which reveals his gums, reminding Lancelot of the features of bald chimpanzees, which, as a boy, he used to go and watch at the zoo, though at the time he did not know whether they were showing their teeth to announce hostility or to signal friendly intentions).

It's odd that Irina told me you were dead... Did you fall out?

The old man sighs, looks outside and says:

It's incredible how much it snows in your part of the world. Round me we can have whole winters without a hint of snow.

Lancelot thinks, OK, OK, you're not answering my questions... well, what are you hoping to find here then?

So (Lancelot, as he usually does, weighs his words), you were saying that you read the report on Irina's accident in the paper...

Yes, yes, yes... and two or three little things seemed suspect...

The man coughs and Lancelot thinks, Now we're getting there.

Irina's father goes on:

First the autopsy. And everything else too (a sweeping hand gesture encapsulating something Lancelot is not equipped to imagine).

I don't understand, says Lancelot, slightly defensively, I didn't read the articles about the accident... I wanted to avoid that sort of writing... (Lancelot adds for his own benefit, Why am I talking to him like this, why have I put on this affected air? The man's comment has launched him straight back into the Very Big Additional Shock, the information Detective Schneider gave him a few days ago, the doubts she sowed in the labyrinth of his pain.) He starts again more calmly, The police referred to some shady questions in the autopsy (he immediately regrets his words when he sees his father-in-law leaning forwards and eyeing him with new interest). But nothing really litigious either...

What proof does he actually have that this man really is Irina's father? He gave in to sentimentality, thinking their eyes had something in common, and all of a sudden he is far less convinced of this symmetry, he looks at the man, terrified to think he has let him into his home (there are so many stories about this sort of thing, you offer them tea and they savagely slit your throat and cart the body away in a bin bag), he starts peering at his face in such a way that Irina's father arches his eyebrows in astonishment.

What's going on? he asks, surprised.

The old man touches his face as if reassuring himself it is the right consistency.

Is something wrong?

Lancelot stands up.

I'm not really myself, please excuse me, could you come back a little later so we can chat about all this more comfortably...

Lancelot bows slightly at his guest and smiles at him, the other man cannot help but take his leave, he stands up too, gives a little cough, wants to arrange another time, hesitates, shifting from one foot to the other, which only adds to his

VÉRONIQUE OVALDÉ

simian qualities in Lancelot's eyes, he rubs his hands together, prevaricates, Lancelot moves closer, takes him by the shoulder and says in his ear:

Leave me alone, I need peace and quiet at the moment.

Lancelot feels there are two of him again and the two Lancelots stand on either side of Irina's father and escort him to the door. When they are about to close the door behind Irina's father, who is already walking off in the snow along the path marked out by one of the Lancelots, the two of them open the door wide again and call out to him. The man turns round questioningly.

Are you staying in the area? Lancelot asks, returning to his body.

I'm at the Central Hotel.

He pauses and adds:

You can find me there.

A crow comes to land between them, it walks with a waddle, placing its feet carefully on the white ground as if not at all sure how stable it is, then it caws before flying off again.

Lancelot feels exhausted. He wants to stay on his island, not to know anything about his wife, his sweetness, his inseparable, not to try to break through the mysteries of any of her lies, I want to shut that room and lock the door, Lancelot waves to Irina's father, Doctor Epstein's pill makes him listless and calm, I want to shut the room and lock the door, he retreats into the house, leaving the winter outside and leaving Irina's father to go back to his car on the bank (a

60

grey Japanese car with fishing rods in the boot and perhaps the old man talks to his wife who can no longer speak, he talks to her, he pretends she's sitting next to him on the passenger seat, he talks to her and goes back to his hotel to empty the mini-bar and watch cable TV, his wife is shut away inside herself and his daughter is dead, this man is thin and rigid and light as the sort of bark they make boats from), Lancelot leans back against the front door and looks over the living room, his armchair and the coffee table, he thinks to himself that the television programme paused there dates back to before Irina's death and the thought makes his head spin, he knows the telephone is going to ring, that the police will call back and ask stupid pernicious questions, he'll wonder, What is it they suspect? He won't be able to see what's going on (thank you, Doctor Epstein), he'll try to concentrate but will get caught up in the quagmire of his nightmare (like in those dreams where he has trouble grasping situations, and when he starts to understand, they've already run through his fingers, they've altered and escaped his analysis, he's always trying to cling on to disappearing things but his feet are caught in treacle which stretches cloyingly as he moves), Lancelot tells himself, I must do something before that fucking phone starts ringing again, before someone else pitches up here saying, Hello, I'm Irina's hidden son.

I could call the police station, he thinks, to check whether Irina's father really is Irina's father. But he does not like the idea. I'm not going to touch the phone or the TV, I'm going to go and make cakes. Lancelot thinks about what his mother used to say about cooking, she always said, It empties my head. This little phrase soothes him, he turns towards the kitchen and decides not to talk to anyone (but what does he mean by anyone – it can only be the police, Lancelot has no friends, that was a choice, a decision, an exclusivity), so he will talk to no one about the sudden arrival of Irina's father.

ELEVEN

Lancelot starts rummaging through recipes to find something to keep his four hands and his two heads-full-of-Irina occupied. He comes across the folder where she put cooking ideas – in fact Irina cooked fairly little for someone who so scrupulously saved recipes from magazines, filed the ones she was given and wrote down the ones dictated to her. Lancelot sits down. He opens the folder. Irina's writing is all over the place, she wrote recipes on anything she could find, the inside of biscotte packets, the back of an envelope. Some of the recipes must date back to when she was very young, a time when she still had to make a note that you recognize boiling water by waiting for 'big bubbles + plop plop'. Lancelot arranges them in piles, he reads them, hoping to unearth something personal, an amusing remark, a date, anything. And that is when, stuck between recipes for *brandade* of cod and chicken curry (harvested in the days before she was a vegetarian), written in Irina's handwriting (big letters leaning to the right with the horizontal bars of Ts acting as roofs for other letters), that is when he stumbles across the recipe for napalm.

One third tonic water + two thirds petrol.

He rereads it. Underneath, in smaller letters, it says: Tonic water or concentrated orange juice.

He says to himself, That's an unusual cocktail.

And he moves on to something else.

He moves on to a meringue-topped redcurrant tart. There aren't any redcurrants round here, he thinks. Could I make the thing with frozen blueberries? He ponders this. Then he turns back to the piece of paper with the un-orthodox recipe for napalm. He reads it again. And affirms, That's a very odd cocktail. He corrects himself, Not one you could *drink* with two thirds petrol. He looks up. Looks above the chest of drawers and thinks, How strange, there was a clock here before, between the poster for old-fashioned chicory and the table summarizing the carbohydrate content of manufactured foods. Lancelot stands there per-plexed, in suspense, he feels as if he is caught in a shower of ashes inside a little snow-scene, the flakes swirling around him every time an unkind – or malicious – hand tips up the ball and its Pompeiian landscape. Lancelot scrutinizes the empty space above the chest of drawers on the watermelon-pink wall that Irina painted herself last winter. He does not remember taking the clock down. He groans, Is it starting again? He tells himself he'll have to be very careful in everything he does, as if being watched by a jittery sniper lying in wait opposite. It's important, he then thinks, to behave as if you're constantly under surveillance by a madman armed to the teeth, it helps you avoid all superfluous gesticulations. Lancelot looks back down at the old sheet of paper. He feels excited, guilty and anxious all at once, like coming across the private diary of a pretty older cousin when he was twelve years old. He reads on: Replace the amylacetate with banana juice. He reads: Replace the potassium chlorate with salt substitute. He reads: Replace the hydrogen peroxide with hair dye. He reads: Replace the sodium hydroxide with washing powder. He reads: Smoke bomb, wrap ping-pong ball in foil then set light (there is a sketch explaining how to hold the device while it burns). He reads: Chlorine bomb = swimming pool chlorine + milk + airtight bottle (NB not glass). He reads: Molotov cocktail = beer bottle + 220 ml alcohol + 80 ml oil + dipped cloth (if fuse make hole in lid). He reads: Acetone peroxide = 6% oxygenated water + acetone + 30% hydrochloric acid (easy).

He could go on reading like this for a long time, both sides of the piece of paper are covered with these formulae. There are stars next to each recipe. Lancelot wonders whether they refer to the degree of difficulty, the scale of damage produced or the number of times Irina tried each formula.

This idea makes him smile.

It is like allowing himself an indecent thought about her... Lancelot contemplates the piece of paper, he thinks they might just be little decorative additions, those stars in blue pen punctuating the white page like grains of rice on the tarmac after a wedding. Or they could be a secret message.

Lancelot holds on to the kitchen table with both hands. He has lost track of his lines of reasoning. He hangs on and eventually decrees that all the formulae he has found are verbal expressions of Irina's exasperation.

He is pleased with his invention: verbal expressions of Irina's exasperation. It sounds real, it's got legs, it roars. He pronounces the words very clearly, Verbal expressions of Irina's exasperation.

Then all of a sudden he is weighed down by a feeling of dejection.

A nasty little voice whispers to him that Irina might have thrown herself off the bridge to be rid of him. Lancelot usually has little trouble covering himself in a blanket of melancholy and regret as if diving beneath a shroud of snow.

So he smooths out the paper, contemplates NAPALM, written out and underlined.

He says to himself, Let's recap.

He says to himself, What's all this juvenile rubbish?

He says to himself, I'm going to put this to one side, and he is thinking as much about the incriminating piece of paper as about the suspicion that's trying to worm its way inside him.

Then he remembers who his wife was. He remembers

her face. He has a special trick for remembering it. He starts with the left eye, then he does the eyebrow and the ear, and the rest appears. The face puts itself together again. He is afraid soon he will not remember Irina's face so clearly, he would like her to have worn glasses, would like to be able to remember her face around an accessory, and for her face, the memory of her face, to have become that accessory. Lancelot panics at the thought of forgetting Irina's face.

And he cannot reconcile his beloved's features with the piece of paper he has just found. Then he says out loud, I've got to ring her father.

He calls directory enquiries then rings the Central Hotel. Clamping the receiver against his shoulder, he turns on the music system, it is *Tosca*, he switches it off, sits on the sofa worn from Irina's reading, gets straight back up and, when he is put through to Irina's father, Lancelot introduces himself and launches right in with:

Prove to me that you really are Irina's father (as he says these words Lancelot feels strong and cunning, like Philip Marlowe).

The other man hesitates for a few seconds, he does not seem impressed, just irritated, the television can be heard very quietly in the background, it is not hard to imagine the man, all thin and stiff, lying on his bed, no more able to bend than a stick of wood, it is easy to picture the orange candlewick bedspread and yellow net curtains, the TV raised up like in a hospital and the man's gaping bag left on the metal stool by the door, Lancelot thinks to himself, My God, I'm here and there at the same time.

I can – the man on the other end of the line articulates slowly – I can show you my identity papers, I can tell you about her, I can show you pictures of her as a child…

Have you got any with you?

I always have them on me.

Lancelot can tell he is not going to last long without sobbing. He runs his hand over his eyes and forehead and says:

When can I see you?

The other man pauses, it sounds as if he turns the volume up on the television, then the sound drops again and he says:

I'm going fishing near the bridge tomorrow morning.

Lancelot thinks to himself, The man's mad, he's going fishing in the river where his daughter drowned. The other man goes on:

Would you like to come with me?

Lancelot thinks, Arsehole, I really don't want to go and freeze to death with you on the banks of the Omoko.

Tomorrow morning's fine, Lancelot accepts (but it is not really him saying these words), eight o'clock at the Omoko bridge.

I'll be there well before then, the other man says calmly, sounding as if he is chewing something, the tinned peanuts from the mini-bar perhaps.

Well, seven o'clock then, says Lancelot (and he knows that if the other man insisted, he would be there straight away, then they could each gauge their attachment to the dead woman they have in common).

Seven o'clock, Irina's father repeats, his voice slightly strangulated by the position of his neck against the pillow. And he hangs up with no further ado, putting the receiver very slowly back on the base as if trying not to hurt it.

TWELVE

The fact that Irina slept with him the moment she sensed he wanted to, that she did not appear to attach much importance to it, that it seemed to be something which happened to her body but not altogether to her, that she felt isolated inside her head and that her body was just a decorative appendage… the way she cohabited with her own flesh, had plunged Lancelot into a state of anxiety for a long time.

For, if she attached so little value to it, she could let anyone use it as she saw fit.

He once voiced the thought, the idea that she granted such paltry importance to her own body that she could never have fucked for money. She looked a bit shocked to know he was thinking that sort of thing. She considered the question. Yes, yes, she said eventually, I've often fucked just out of courtesy. To thank someone for a favour, for example. For giving me a lift from one place to another. For asking me out to dinner. But never directly for money.

Lancelot watched her thinking – she was on the sofa, gazing into space, curled up on herself with a blanket over her legs, and she shifted imperceptibly as if fully to appreciate the comfort and warmth of this configuration. He thought to himself, Christ, please make her stop sleeping with just anybody, he started imagining her with other men, taking her in various different positions, his face tensed, the lewd little film in his head was making him gag, he grimaced and said to himself, I think I've drunk a whole spoonful of vinegar, and she turned towards him, That's all over now, my love, I don't want people doing that to my body any more.

And Lancelot felt very sad hearing her say those words, he went over to her, he found her touching, that is what he told himself, She's touching, he felt like crying, he thought, Whatever is happening to me, it must be something to do with my mother (Lancelot sometimes rebuffed himself like this to curtail his natural sensitivity), he would have so loved it if Irina had reassured him, had signed a piece of paper, there and then, committing herself to no longer lending her body (she had even used the words, Men made use of it temporarily, as if talking about handing a tin opener over to her neighbour or sub-letting her apartment in the summer) to every last priapic bastard who came her way.

He took her in his arms, she smiled as if she understood she was the one who needed to console him, and rocked him in silence for a long time.

Afterwards she got up with a sigh and said, I feel fat. And

Lancelot looked up at her (he was sitting on the rug next to the sofa) and said what he thought she was hoping for, You're not, you're not fat at all.

She turned round and frowned at him, Oh, because you know about that sort of thing, I suppose?

He felt uncomfortable, he seemed to remember having the same sort of conversation as a teenager – which was completely wrong, given that as a teenager he was so frightened of girls that none of them would have come and complained to him about the circumference of her thighs, all they did was ignore him and look at him from afar as if he belonged to a different species. He had often felt slightly repulsive (Am I sweating?) or contagious (Have I got warts?). At the time Lancelot thought this ill-favour was specific to him, he was still unaware of the fundamental laws governing relations between girls and boys, never guessing that his reserve, slight short-sightedness and apparent detachment gave him an aura all his own. Irina said, Sorry, and he repeated it, Sorry. They smiled at each other and she said, Even so, I feel like a whale at the moment. He held out his hand to her and said, It's weird, women always want to be the thinnest person around. She smiled again and closed the subject, Don't worry, I can cope with my disappointments.

THIRTEEN

Lancelot keeps taking his pills, the ones that are meant to tranquillize him and make him think only insipid thoughts through a baby-pink filter. These pills fight off obsessions. That was what Doctor Epstein said, They'll help you fight off your obsessions, and Lancelot wondered what he meant, whether the despair he felt thinking his treasure no longer existed was in any way obsessive. He did not dare ask, but just told himself, Doctor Epstein knows what he's doing.

He keeps taking his pills, he must hang on till seven o'clock tomorrow morning, then he studies the contents of the medicine cabinet, finds a box of out-of-date Valium (he was unaware she even took that sort of thing), there are three left and he swallows them with a bit of water from the bathroom tap, he goes back downstairs and very soon feels exhausted, overwhelmed by a drunken sleepiness (Irina was the one who drank, not him), he starts laughing and his laugh makes his shoulders shake, he goes Oh oh oh, and the syllables stretch and sound something like, Oooooh

Oooooh Oooooh, and he ends up falling asleep on the concrete floor of the garage, with his arms spread wide to form a cross. He wakes several hours later (it is now dark), frozen and with the terrifying impression that a nest of tarantulas have taken up residence in his brain, crawling around, spinning silken thread, venomous. He sits there in the dark, surrounded by all the wooden crates where he keeps his tools and writes the contents of each one on it with a marker pen. Lancelot is an assiduous man, he feels all this meticulousness living around him, he is almost assaulted by it, as if there were heaps of ashes and microscopic bones arranged in urns lined up along the shelves of a columbarium, the darkness soothes his pain (his neck is stiff, his head and feet cold) but nurtures his ramblings. He would like to stay sitting down, his arse frozen on the dusty concrete of the garage, for the rest of his life. He has a feeling of total isolation. His grief feels as palpable as the strong-smelling black air around him (it smells of mildew and petrol, it smells of old rubber going crumbly and sticky). Lancelot breathes slowly as if to avoid ill-treating his lungs, and thinks he has nothing better to do than cry over what is no more. Which he does. And he stays there a good hour, dazed, sobbing but not moving, in his garage. Eventually he calms down and wonders, Maybe I won't be able to get up, and, unable to bear not talking any longer and because he never hears a voice all day except on the radio or the detective calling with details and suspicions, he says out loud, Maybe

I'm paralysed. Hearing the sound of his own voice does him a lot of good. He utters the words, Right, I've got to get out of here. And he gets up, his head spins slightly but he gets over to the door which leads to the staircase, and as he goes up the stairs, as he holds on to the banister (which is just a wooden curtain rail that he screwed there, thinking it would only be temporary), he cries out, What the hell did she see in me? For God's sake, what did she see in me?

Halfway up the stairs Lancelot stops. He asks himself, one foot in the air, he says to himself, The middle of a staircase is the perfect place to look for answers. He thinks, Why did she always go to the ends of the earth to film all those doomed animals? What was she chasing?

If Lancelot ever asked her this, she would twirl round and say, I'm chasing time, which just keeps marching on. Then she smirked as if to make sure he did not take her words at face value.

Lancelot is still asking himself questions and has now sat down on the stairs, holding the wall with one hand as if to make sure there are no subsidence problems threatening.

Irina's youth was shrinking away and the Gorgons were gradually turning her travels into a sort of multi-storey parking area for disappointments, despondency and exhaustion.

Lancelot realizes that journeys have always filled him with despair, making intense feelings of dejection well up inside him – didn't all journeys lead to a lagoon half filled with deep water and toxic weeds, where the mists were bound to be clammy and the true taste of the world always inaccessible? Lancelot sniggers, gets up and starts climbing again. He is determined to get all the way up these stairs, even if he has to do it on all fours. He reaches the landing. But as he sets foot in their bedroom, still moaning to himself, What could she have seen in someone like me? he starts beating a retreat because the sight of their bed chokes him and knocks him sideways.

And there is something else.

Irina's dressing table is no longer there. It was definitely here in the left-hand corner of the room, let's gather our thoughts, not lose our heads, it was definitely still here two days ago or a week, then, or I don't know, or could Irina have given it away to the Salvation Army? No, she obviously didn't do anything like that, the dressing table has just disappeared, that is one constant in Lancelot's life, objects tipping into a parallel dimension, he can do nothing about it.

He goes back down to the living room, clinging to the wall, switches on the television which, very fortuitously, has not turned into a ghost, and settles into his armchair to watch a boxing match, soon falling asleep in its spasmodic glow, intoxicated by the commentary that sounds so like a litany he believes he is listening to a prayer.

FOURTEEN

It is no longer dark when Lancelot stops near the Omoko bridge. The sky is already turning red in the east but he does not feel this reddening will succeed in setting anything alight. Lancelot stays sitting in his car watching this phenomenon, turns off the radio, which is broadcasting a programme about insomnia, listens to the car clicking and cooling and thinks, This must be what sunrise looks like at the North Pole.

Then he gets out and slams the door, and the sound it makes as it shuts is hollow and metallic, perfectly attuned to the frozen surface of the world. Lancelot looks around and thinks, The man's stood me up, a thought that relieves and depresses him (now he can get back home into the warm but there will be no one there to greet him). That is when he notices the grey Japanese car parked behind the electricity huts on the other side of the bridge. He goes over, hands thrust in his pockets, exhaling a cloud of water vapour with every breath. He looks at the surrounding area, imagining the police watching him and wondering what he is up to on the Omoko bridge at dawn, and he thinks he should have warned them that Irina's father has turned up, then scoffs at himself. You're a very disciplined submissive sort of person, Irina once told him, stroking his face. And he found those words horrible, he thought she could easily have described a pony like that as she tickled the animal's head.

He can smell the sweat on his body cooling and evaporating.

He shivers.

The bridge is a ghostly place.

All this clear air and my see-through heart.

Lancelot leans against the patched-up parapet.

Did she think about me as it all came to an end?

A very distinctive kind of cold seems to come up off the river, an earthy sort of cold, damp and mentholated.

When I was with Irina I never felt loneliness the way I do now. It stops me breathing and picturing what's going to happen in the hours ahead. It's keeping me stuck in the present. Tarring my feathers.

Lancelot shakes himself and peels himself away from the parapet.

As he walks towards his father-in-law's Japanese car, he wonders when everything started getting out of hand. He thinks it was connected to their leaving Camerone for this icy place. Lancelot can now see it was an absurd choice. Swapping Camerone and its easy climate for the harsh one here… In the end they only lived in Camerone for nine months before Irina cajoled him into finally agreeing they should exchange her old apartment for the shingle-roofed house in the middle of the snow. I can't cope with this town and its pollution any more, she announced, I'm suffocating, suffocating. And she pretended to choke. And Lancelot thought, At least I'd have her all to myself there. And that was a very bad reason to leave. Lancelot was well aware of it. Still, that was the reason that drove him out of his usual mineral inertia and into organizing their move to Catano…

At this stage in his reflections Lancelot spots the man at the foot of the bridge, on the bank, behind a rock, standing with a fishing rod in his hand, smoking, apparently lost in contemplating his float or the current dragging limp weeds along, he is dressed the same as the day before, and Lancelot thinks to himself, He looks young from here, how old can he have been when he had Irina? The man looks up and waves at Lancelot, who heads over to him down the steep slope. There are almost two metres of ice stretching away from the bank but the middle of the river is still free-flowing. Lancelot tells himself, It's not all that cold, but even so I'm chilled to the bone. Hello, he calls out to the man. The latter responds with a nod (so as not to frighten the fish?).

Lancelot tries not to look at the river straight away.

Irina died in there, he tells himself.

But she did not actually.

Irina did not die in there.

And Lancelot knows that. The police informed him of it. Detective Schneider eventually announced that, in all probability, she was dead before she ended up in the middle of the river in the car. (Whose car, incidentally, remind me who the car belonged to? Oh, you haven't found out yet? Let me know when you know the name of the person whose car my wife died in, yes yes yes, let me know, I really would be very grateful.)

Irina did not drown.

Hearing that was a Very Big Additional Shock.

For now there are too many tiles missing from the mosaic so Lancelot finds it difficult to conceive of Irina's death as anything other than a drowning. He is still inclined to look at the river as if its waters had served to fill his beloved's lungs (her ears and mouth and every orifice), and finds it quite hard to bear. He sees the car fall and his princess's hair rippling in the water as it rises inside the vehicle, it is her hair he can picture, her heavy eyelids lowered, the fabric of her coat growing heavier and swelling with all that river water, and he can imagine Irina's hair dancing about her face, no longer curly as it was in real life, but long and supple and light and vegetal, it all seems very slow, not at all fervent or bloody or noisy or quick, there is no impact, of aluminium or iron, no noise, it is a silent, romantic drowning that Lancelot pictures, with just the delicate sound of air bubbles rising up around Irina's body, enveloping it, delineating it but no longer able to help it,

Lancelot watches this slow-motion sequence, Irina is weightless now, she has become a sylph, her hands drift up above her head as if she were offended by all this black water surrounding and penetrating her. The car reaches the sandy riverbed, raising small sterile eddies which remind Lancelot of the astronauts' footsteps when they landed on the moon, everything goes out, the car headlights flicker and admit defeat, it is now completely dark in the surrounding river water and inside Irina.

The film stops.

Lancelot finds his feet again.

He comes up to Irina's father.

He would like to look casual but it is impossible in this cold. He jumps about on the spot, the other man turns towards him and stares at Lancelot's feet, making him understand that his jumping is driving the fish away, so he stops and his teeth start chattering.

My name's Paco, the man announces.

And I'm Lancelot (Lancelot realizes he never knew Irina's father's name).

Paco nods to show he knows this, and goes back to his contemplation. Lancelot thinks to himself, This is ridiculous, he was the one who came to see me and now he's not talking. He swallows two capsules he has been keeping in his jacket pocket and says to himself, Relax.

He looks at the big flat imprisoned bubbles through the translucent ice, they sometimes move very quickly then stop dead as if trying to find the most strategic place, he can hear jackdaws, and cars crossing the bridge, he thinks about Irina's father's name, it means nothing to him, he thinks, That's Spanish, isn't it, Paco? He tries to think but his whole mind is taken up with constant fog, so, to get rid of the horrible bogged-down feeling, he eventually says:

She wasn't actually meant to be on the Omoko bridge that evening. I'd taken her to the airport myself. I went home and, quarter of an hour before the police called, she rang me to tell me her flight to Sri Lanka was delayed.

In the middle of the night?

In the middle of the night.

She was supposed to be flying in the middle of the night?

Yes (Lancelot turns to face the man and frowns).

Planes don't take off at night.

Ah.

Lancelot stares at the opposite bank and nods his head, he feels terribly weary, infinitely saddened that she did not bother to make her lie credible, that she knew Lancelot was so far removed from the real world that he would not know even this simple fact. He looks at Paco and realizes the other man must think him a twit.

So?

What? Lancelot manages.

What do you think? What do the police think?

I don't know. I think she had a double life (he has trouble saying this, Lancelot does, it sticks in his throat).

A lover?

Maybe.

Paco does not press the point. He studies his float.

What are you fishing for? Lancelot asks.

Trout.

Lancelot catches himself in time, he was about to say he likes trout with flaked almonds, he feels dismayed, thinking, I'm losing the plot. The man beside him still looks like a retired soldier and his stiff bearing makes Lancelot nervous.

What did she tell you I died of? Irina's father asks all of a sudden.

Actually, it wasn't very clear... Drink... Something like that...

Really?

Yes.

I'm amazed she didn't invent something more... twisted... (and here Lancelot thinks, Is he talking about Irina or someone else?) struck down by lightning, eaten away by testicular cancer, or steeped in concrete by a gang of crooks paid by the Russian mafia.

I don't think she would have dreamt up things like that, Lancelot ventures cautiously.

Really? the other man responds and glances sideways at Lancelot, who thinks to himself, He's trying to suggest he knows her better than me, he thinks I'm the gullible idiot in this whole performance.

Lancelot needs to sit down. His legs are giving way, he suddenly feels dominated by this man and by Irina, he wonders, Was I manipulated? He says to himself, My darling, my treasure, my sweetheart.

And what else? Irina's father asks.

What do you mean?

Do the police just think she had a double life?

Yes, why? Were you thinking there was something else?

Oh no, no, no, I wasn't thinking anything. I just wondered what's bothering them, given that her having a double life is really more your business, it's up to you to get your head round that now.

Lancelot watches the float bobbing with the current, the weeds drifting along the line, and eventually says:

You see, she didn't drown. She was already dead when the car went into the river.

Ah. Ah (it could have sounded like him clearing his throat or a little laugh).

For now they're suggesting a heart attack, Lancelot explains.

And you?

She didn't have a heart problem as far as I know, but (sweeping hand movement through the air as if his fingers are burning and he needs to cool them) it seems I didn't know her all that well.

Yes. It seems so.

Lancelot thinks, Fuck it, I'm the one who can say that,

you prick, you have absolutely no right to suggest that sort of thing.

Then he says to himself, I'm busy giving information to this guy when he's standing there like a moron trying to strike a trout and he knows much more than I do on the subject of Irina.

Tell me about her when she was a child, he asks.

Irina's father looks at the sky, he extinguishes his cigarette in a metal box brought along for the purpose, there are already half a dozen stubs inside it, Lancelot thinks he wouldn't like to be an ant shut in there, it must stink. Paco screws the lid back on, puts the box away in his bag and starts:

She was the sweetest little girl. She was very good. She spent a lot of time going to mass with her mother. And otherwise she drew stuff with Jesus and the apostles and Mary Magdalene and the angel Gabriel, her room was covered in them. She used to say she wanted to be a nun. Irina sang in church, she had the clearest voice in the world. Her mother was away a lot. She had depression. She would go off for sleeping cures. And it made Irina very angry. Irina cooked my meals and took care of everything while her mum was away. And she prayed the whole time, because she was angry and for her mother's 'salvation'. When her mum came home Irina used to hide her pills. She'd heard the priest say antidepressants were 'the devil's own sweetmeats'. That went on until boys took over all the space in her heart.

Which happened when?

When she was fourteen fifteen.

Did everything change?

She never went to church again and at seventeen she ended up running away with the boy she was seeing at the time, a guy who worked on a chicken farm. They left by car with a cool box in the boot and about a dozen frozen chickens. We didn't see her for two years. Her mother was so messed up...

Didn't you try to find her?

She was seventeen, it wouldn't have been much good forcing her to come back home only for her to curse everyone for another eight months and then clear off again with her chicken killer.

That's one way of looking at things.

Paco turns slowly towards Lancelot and the latter feels convinced that a slender forked tongue is about to dart from his father-in-law's mouth, and he is going to bury his venom-laden fangs in his neck. Lancelot says to himself, It's incredible how like a cobra the guy looks.

In the end he asks:

What did she do for two years?

She tried all sorts of things, she learned to make films, that was what she wanted to do, she did a bit of trafficking with the chicken boyfriend...

Trafficking?

At the time he started working in a hospital, he would raid

AND MY SEE-THROUGH HEART

the central infirmary (Paco shakes his head as if the whole business is coming back to him with migraine-inducing clarity). But not for drugs, no, he swiped bandages, catheters, electrocardiographs… and Irina peddled them with him.

Irina?

She sent quite a lot of the stuff to Africa or Asia or I don't really know where, they were in cahoots with alternative, politically dubious organizations which supported various rioting factions lying low around the world.

No?

Well, yes. They also had links with associations that took care of the homeless and people in substandard housing. Then they started nicking bigger stuff, wheelchairs, transparent cribs for newborns, next they launched into beds and metal cupboards. It was a Robin Hood sort of thing. Redistributing wealth. In the end they were nabbed.

No?

It nearly cost them everything. But they had a couple of strategic connections, political support, and they wangled their way out of it without too much damage. That said, he adds after a moment's thought, it's not like it stopped them.

I can't get over it, Lancelot blurts, staring at the surface of the river.

A remark he makes more for his own benefit than Paco's, but the latter turns to him and fires this at him:

I don't understand. Didn't she talk to you? Didn't she tell you anything? Didn't she trust you?

I thought she did.

Lancelot descends into profound silence. He feels sad and abandoned. This is what he was always afraid of. That Irina would abandon him. Lancelot sighs:

I think I'm going to sell the house and go back to town. I can't see myself staying round here on my own.

His musings do not seem to interest Irina's father, who does not even bother to nod or grunt. So Lancelot says, I'm off, and he starts to head back towards the slope, the other man says nothing, does not wave, perhaps he thinks that someone who knew his daughter so little is not worthy of being called a man. Lancelot still feels just as sad but angry too, he says to himself, Family of crackpots, fucking family of crackpots. He climbs the slope and goes back to the verge along the road. He catches his breath with both hands on his knees, clenches his teeth, then hurries back to his car, where he can shut himself away and cry in peace with the heating on.

FIFTEEN

So Irina is like a firefly. A frazzled firefly. A feeble crackling sound and the light goes out.

What's left of Irina, then, in her little metal box?

SIXTEEN

Lancelot sometimes feels like a dinosaur. With about as much grace and intelligence as those great hulks. Besides, he is convinced he lives according to some archaic system that has not been in force for a few million years.

For example, to Lancelot, words mean something.

He believes in vows, keeps his promises, makes a wish every time he eats his first cherry of the season – he thought he would never be able to leave Elisabeth because he was married to her, it took meeting someone like Irina (who could make you abandon quite a few of your convictions) to cast doubt on that irrefutable situation.

It may well be that Lancelot attaches too much importance to words. He takes everything so literally.

As soon as he gets home from his miserable meeting with Irina's father he calls the estate agents and puts the house on the market. The woman who runs the agency is called Marie Marie, which Lancelot finds completely astonishing. Then he remembers why he is called Lancelot – his mother read a medieval epic when she was pregnant. So he feels some solidarity with Marie Marie and her stammering name.

When Marie Marie turns up at Lancelot's house, he makes a cup of tea and is surprised to find himself thinking she is pretty – a thought that plunges him into a state of abject distress, he takes two blue capsules and says to himself, My Irina, my treasure, my little pussy. Marie Marie is wearing a pink suit, she changed into high-heeled pink shoes on the doorstep, leaving her snow-laden clodhoppers outside, and she was still perched on one foot like a flamingo when he opened the door to her. She gave him a very apologetic smile and Lancelot thought to himself, She's delightful (Lancelot likes girls in distress, girls who are touching, girls who are pretty but faintly ridiculous, he likes girls when they are just slightly vulgar and flashy, he is so grateful to them for the effort they put into seduction).

Lancelot thinks of his mother, who was always alone and over made-up. He sighs inwardly at the thought that this Marie Marie should make him think of his mother, and says to himself, I'm a sentimental fool, but cannot help super-imposing his mother's face on the woman from the agency.

As she goes into the living room she adopts an awkward expression which she thinks is appropriate. Her pink suit is not the right thing at all. She knows about Irina's death, and would like to appear moved, but the effectiveness of her modest expression is belied by her finery, there is a sort of discrepancy with that pink suit, she must be annoyed with herself for choosing it this morning, she must have had nothing else that was clean, or did not sleep at home and had no time to nip back and change, so here she is pitching up to meet this grieving man dressed like a giant peony.

Lancelot realizes it may be his happy pills that are dressing Miss Marie Marie in the whole pink get-up. She might just be some poor girl who has been turned into a bombshell by the chemicals.

Lancelot wonders, Does she really look the way I see her here, isn't my grief blinding me? He thinks, Behind the sickly perfume she's giving off isn't there an acrid, slightly sweet, repulsive smell of pumpkins? This is a witch who's come into my house, isn't it, having left her besom broom with her boots by the door, and using all that candy pink to pass herself off as an estate agent? Is she into black magic and trying to send me to sleep by being trivial and awkward?

He registers that she is smiling at him and that the smile has been hovering on her face for too long, she finds him attractive, Lancelot can hardly believe it, he never could, he has always had so much trouble seeing himself as attractive. Irina used to say, You're a good-looking man, you do know that, don't you? And she always seemed to wonder whether he denied his assets out of coquetry or because he did not recognize his own strengths and charm. She used to study him suspiciously with a furrow in her brow which meant 'don't give me that'.

I knew your wife, Miss Marie Marie says. She used to pop into the agency to say hello… (Lancelot, who has sat down opposite her, watches her, lurking behind his cup of tea.) Until a month ago she was still looking for a house for the two of you, she would come in and look at the details and view houses.

Lancelot does not want to look like a husband who is unaware of his wife's house-moving activities, he gives a smile that fails to crease his eyes, like the cat in Alice in Wonderland, all that is missing are the stripes, he thinks to himself, I've had enough, I don't understand any of it, it's all so exhausting. Then he pulls himself together and replies:

I'd really like to see the last house she viewed.

Ooooh (a cry that sounds something like an ecstatic shrew), of course, Mr Rubinstein (she must be one of those people who think Rubinstein is Jewish and that Jews are rich), the minute I get back to the office I'll check availability and I'll take you there… (Lancelot finds her less and less appealing… that often happens… he is charmed by their little-match-girl look, then finds out they are grasping teasers.)

She gets up, asks permission to take a few photographs, walks through the rooms, re-positions a few lamps, makes him sign the 'vendor' box on some pieces of paper, asks with all the tact in the world whether he is the sole owner of the house, which he confirms he is, then she twitters, talks about 'micromarkets' and interest rates, Lancelot follows her, he has no desire to leave her alone in any of the rooms, all he wants now is for her to clear off, he notices that the sugary perfume she gives off – the one masking the filthy reek of pumpkins – smells of raspberries, he tells himself it must be her bubble bath, he tells himself, I must air the place when she's gone, he tells himself, I could never sleep with a girl who washes in raspberry-scented crap, then pulls himself together, There's no question of sleeping with her anyway.

He thinks, I don't recognize myself.

When she has finally left he lights a scented candle, it is gloomy and about to snow again, he can feel the cold laying siege to the house, he puts his hand flat against the walls, which seem porous and damp, he thinks to himself he has nothing to do but wait for nightfall. Usually he writes articles for the local paper and reads their proofs, he does it there, *in situ*, in their disgusting, nicotine-stained offices, but at the moment Lancelot has nothing to do, he goes and stands by the window, crosses his arms and looks up at the car headlights in the distance sweeping through the gathering darkness, he wonders, How many daylight hours are there left? It feels like the night is gaining ground every day, he thinks of Irina, of her shoulders, her breasts and her pussy, it is very painful, it pinches and twists, like a knee ligament which reminds you it is there with every step, making you flinch forwards. Lancelot thinks, I hope she didn't fake it, a slow non-lethal venom spreads through his veins and irrigates his organs, Lancelot loved fucking with Irina, he felt he had never done it before meeting her, It's incredible this exists, he used to think, and I didn't even know about it till now. Before Irina he had had an obscure second-hand knowledge of the thing, he had coped very well without it, mind you, had adapted, it didn't bother him at all, he couldn't give a stuff that he didn't regularly make use of his dick, it didn't call anything into question because he didn't think about it, as if he had put sex and everything that went with it into a tightly sealed box, put the box in the freezer and thought no more about it. It was certainly very comfortable. When he met Irina, he realized it was not possible to forget part of yourself like that. It's not normal, she told him.

And standing there by the window, waiting for the snow to start falling again, Lancelot thinks he wants to die he misses her so much. It hits him in the solar plexus. Like a punch or a dumdum bullet, shattering his breastbone. This is going to be difficult, he says cautiously (his voice echoes oddly, as if bouncing off something soft) and he takes another couple of pills. The depth of silence, which always precedes a fall of snow, drains the energy from his legs, crushes them like a millstone. He thinks to himself, This must be how cold and dark and silent it feels in outer space. Then sneers grimly.

He is waiting for the telephone to ring.

The telephone starts ringing – Lancelot is developing a knowledge of things beyond him, he seems to be able to predict certain minor incidents.

Lancelot walks away from the window and picks up.

Mr Rubinstein? the pink thingy from the estate agents chirps (just before picking up the phone, Lancelot would have wagered his house that it was the pink thingy from the agency calling).

Yes.

About the house that your wife (brief pause intended to express distress) viewed, I could take you there tomorrow (the tone getting perkier again).

Good news.

I've checked. I didn't have to make an appointment, we've got the keys and it hasn't been inhabited for a while...

Ah.

Shall I pick you up at about one o'clock? (Her voice sounds like little bells you might ring to ward off spirits.)

One o'clock.

Great, see you tomorrow, Mr Rubinstein (or, actually, you could compare this voice to the clinking sound of a couple of dozen gold bangles on a woman's wrist).

See you tomorrow.

Yes yes, see you at one o'clock tomorrow (she repeats the time clearly, a professional).

Lancelot hangs up softly, grimacing, not wanting to destroy any further the incredible silence around him, holding his breath and straining his ears. He says to himself, My life's falling apart. He thinks of the morning of Irina's death, it was a Tuesday, he woke beside her and her body was warm, still sort of full of sleep, with a soft salty smell coming off it, a smell of warm sand, she had her back to him and he put his hand on her hip and she turned towards him and kissed him, she smiled and said, Hello. And Lancelot looks for a sign, something which could have given him an inkling that the day would be the beginning of his great heartache, that right then, early that morning, he was embarking on a dark period, something that could change the course of history. Lancelot says to himself, I started my day by stroking her skin, and he realizes that that just doesn't gel with what happened afterwards, she ended that fateful Tuesday in an unknown car in the depths of the river, and it just doesn't gel.

Lancelot takes up his position by the living-room window again and draws back the curtain, he will stay like that for hours, he may even succeed in staying on his feet, gazing aimlessly at the sky swarming with microscopic grey flakes, until one o'clock the following day.

SEVENTEEN

In his whole life Lancelot has only ever seen one photo of Irina as a child. It lay around in a yellowed envelope among her tax-return forms. In it Irina was wearing big round glasses, a pony tail and a gold crucifix round her neck. She was smiling at the lens, revealing the gaps in her teeth. The picture was full-length. It showed her gumboots which came halfway up her calves, a rounded tummy sticking out from a vest top and green shorts riding up between her legs, which made her look like a pitiful communicant, a little girl who had been raped or a cousin coping with a slight handicap. She had tanned, rounded shoulders. And that was what you couldn't take your eyes off. Her tanned, rounded shoulders. They conflicted with the rest of her. A sort of power struggle. In the picture, Irina was showing the photographer the book she was reading, probably a strip cartoon, but the flash had whitened its pages altogether.

EIGHTEEN

They are in Marie Marie's car – a blue Ford Taurus with crushed wafers in the passenger footwell, a dead dog smell in the back, a worn booster seat, stuffing straggling out of the armrests, and Barbra Streisand as a backing track. Marie Marie twitters away as she drives, she is wearing light pink lipstick outlined with darker pink lip liner, it actually makes her look as if she has a moustache, she bats her eyelids and screws up her eyes, which worries Lancelot, She's hopelessly short-sighted, she's going to send us hurtling into the scenery, but he settles deeper into his seat and thinks, It would probably be for the best.

When they reach the place where the house should be, she brakes, checks the address and says, I don't understand, it should be here. Lancelot smiles at her (his first smile for a long time), she looks like a four-year-old who has put too much water in her glass of squash and watches it overflowing without being able to stop the flood.

She mutters, My God my God my God. Then exclaims, I

think the house no longer exists. She looks panic-stricken, they have just covered fifty kilometres to see a house that no longer exists. And it could either be the time wasted not doing something more lucrative or the astonishment at dipping her toe into a world way beyond her that puts Miss Thingummypink into a state of consternation. She manages, Sweetjesussweetjesussweetjesus. Lancelot looks at her and tells himself, Actually if she hadn't been so keen on pink she would have been a nun. He notices her ring finger, she is wearing a wedding ring, he nods, She's not a nun. Then he suggests, Shall we have a quick look? She parks on the verge but refuses to get out of the car, Lancelot heaves himself from his seat, puts both his feet in the snow and walks over to the fence surrounding what was once a smart house and is now just a large crater. It is a quiet residential area, people are out walking their dogs (but, Lancelot notices, not on this side of the street), others hurry past, wrapping their coats round them as they would a dressing gown after showering, inappropriate people with ties tied, wearing delicate but classy shoes with soles like cigarette papers, clutching to their chests with gloved hands an attaché case incapable of arresting the progress of the cold which is freezing their blood, silently cursing the north wind with a few well-chosen words, and taking small, hasty steps like old widowed aunts worried about breaking a hip. Lancelot peers over the fence, the house seems to have been blown away, or collapsed the way condemned tower blocks in housing estates collapse when they are dynamited. People film them so they can wonder at the miracle of the neighbouring blocks, themselves busy decaying but still standing unperturbed, and later replaced by other equally doomed blocks. Lancelot thinks about those images that people take such pleasure in watching – particularly, Irina used to say, if you were a man. Irina had a theory on the subject. She would say, On the beach little girls decorate sand castles with seashells and little boys kick them down. (Lancelot always thought to himself, Just remind me who built them, though?)

There is nothing left of the house, just an excavation which might lead you to think a meteorite had landed there after its voyage through space, before completely disintegrating. Lancelot wonders what happened to everything that was in the house, can things just volatize like that? Isn't there some business about matter never disappearing but always transforming into something else?

Lancelot goes back to the car and opens the door. Miss Marie Marie is on the phone telling one of her colleagues that the house has vanished into thin air, she speaks with a degree of delight, as if announcing a scoop, a new affair or widespread cancer in some show-biz star. She says, The house has been blown up, then gives a snort and repeats, The house has been blown up. When she hangs up Lancelot asks, Who does the house belong to? He is still standing in the doorway, so she pretends to shiver and squeals, Close that. Lancelot does not move and says again, Who does this house belong to? She hesitates for a moment, then frowns, apparently evaluating the situation, and eventually reaches for her file, which is scudding about in the footwell with the wafers, grumbling, I'll catch my death, as she consults the jumble of papers. Lancelot, beside her, is staggered by her lack of organization, savouring the voluptuous pleasure of pissing her off by leaving the door open and letting some powdery snow land on the pussycat-grey mouldy texture of the seat.

He really wants her to lean towards him. He really wants to close the door on her neck. To break her little poppet's neck with the door. Lancelot can already see something bloody and velvet-smooth dripping on the snow, and himself totally absorbed by it, he knows what her skin will look like when it is no longer irrigated, what her eyes will look like when they are no longer alive, he wants to see her tongue protruding from her lips and going blue, he would throw her dismantled body on the pavement and requisition her car, he would leave the two pieces of Miss Pink Sweetie to empty themselves from all their orifices and sully the snow outside the absent house, and he would take flight, fully appreciating his first murder (and making a wish, of course)…

The owner is a Mr Romero… Marie Marie eventually exhumes from her heap of dog-eared papers.

And what does he do? asks Lancelot, regaining his footing after his blood-soaked fantasy.

In life?

In life.

I don't know. I don't have his profession on here (she waves the piece of paper between two fingers with a hint of disgust).

Could you find out?

Why?

Could you find out? (Lancelot gives her his most charming smile, one that says, I've lost my wife, I'm desperately lonely, be nice and you will be granted your place in paradise.)

Yes (she is reluctant so, to be sure Lancelot fully appreciates the effort she will be going to, she adds), I'm not supposed to give you that sort of information…

It's a pretty exceptional situation, I would say (Lancelot realizes he probably sounds threatening).

She puts her file back down among the wafers.

Shall we go? she says grumpily.

Lancelot does not reply but sits down beside her in a cloud of snow and crumbs while she starts the car.

It's funny the house disappearing, Lancelot thinks to himself. Funny and weird. He tries to remember whether Irina ever mentioned a Romero. He can feel the onset of the familiar pinching, would like to quash it but it does not work.

Did Irina know this man?

Was Irina in this Romero's car when she fell from the

bridge? (Lancelot pictures him as stocky, pot-bellied, elegant, in a black suit and spotless shirt.)

Did Romero extricate himself from the car in the freezing water when it sank in the Omoko, and did he scarper as quickly as he could so no one discovered their affair which could ruin his political career?

In the time it takes to get out of that leafy suburb Lancelot silently invents half a dozen twisted scenarios. Marie Marie starts describing what the house used to look like (the conservatory, the aviary), and tells him to have a look at the details, there are pictures of the interior, his wife absolutely loved it, she assures him, she was hesitating because she felt it might be a bit too big (eight bedrooms) but it really was 'love at first sight'. Marie Marie uses this expression several times. She also repeats three times, A very unusual property. Lancelot looks through the pictures of the aviary, the conservatory, the eight bedrooms and the chandelier in the hall. He wonders, How did Irina take people for a ride like that when she spent half her time filming bears in various mountains around the world (and with that Lancelot thinks, If that was even true, and this suspicion feels like an injection of acid into a still palpitating organ). In the file there is a folder with the words CLIENT DETAILS written across it in huge letters in marker pen. He would like to look at it but it is sealed with several paper clips. He turns towards Marie Marie, suddenly feeling a sense of urgency, while a little phrase spools through his head (*He was the stuff of heroes*, it drums away), and that little phrase plagues him (*He was the stuff of heroes*, like the snatch of a tune heard in the morning which clings to the brain with suction-cup insistence, setting a rhythm to everything you do for hours), he would like to shut the little phrase up (*He was the stuff of heroes*, extraordinary idea, isn't it, a hero like a rag doll), so he asks Marie Marie to try to find some information about Mr Romero's profession right now. She picks up her mobile, calls the agency and asks what this Mr Romero does in life, they say they will call her back, she hangs up and waits in silence with Lancelot for the phone to start trilling again. She emits a series of cadenced sighs while Lancelot tries to silence the fucking little phrase boring through his brain (*He's the stuff-uff-uff of hero-o-oes*). He tells himself, It must have something to do with Doctor Epstein's magic pills, it's like a new sort of migraine, your blood pulsing ridiculous pronouncements which invade your brain and stop you thinking. You can always try listening to the radio, try to anaesthetize yourself by putting music on at top volume, focus on listening to what Marie Marie is on about, impossible to shut up the stupid little voice hammering away in your ears.

The phone starts ringing – *Ode to Joy* on a synthesizer. Marie Marie answers it, makes some noises with her mouth, bends down behind the dashboard thinking she sees a police car at the crossroads, sits back up and hangs up. She announces reluctantly (as if wondering what to ask in exchange for the information), Mr Romero is the director of Promedan Laboratories.

Oh? Lancelot manages.

He wonders whether he is disappointed. As if he were checking the state of his limbs after finding a booby-trap bomb in his dustbin. The drilling little phrase has gone away. Lancelot is relieved. He rests his forehead against the car window, feeling as if these suburbs go on for ever with their opulent houses complete with gates and bells, and pathetic signs, 'Beware lunatic cat' and stuff like that, and intercoms so no one has to walk across the garden in the ruthless arctic climate round here, or to keep out intruders. He travels through all this whiteness in slow motion, imagining everything inside is dead, there is no one in the streets, and inside those kitchens everyone is sprawled on the floor, poisoned, the car drags itself along impossibly slowly, Lancelot looks out of the window and smiles. He thinks, My princess, my treasure, my sweet potato, what did you come here for? Here he is talking to his beloved over and beyond the crematorium. He starts laughing uncontrollably, right there beside Marie Marie, who glances at him suspiciously, but does not want to look stupid and would actually like to be able to laugh with him, because then she would be sure she's not missing anything and that Lancelot Rubinstein isn't busy making fun of her.

Then he says:

I'd like you to sell my house before it goes up in smoke.

She smiles, reassured, thinking he is just having a joke with her.

She says:

Don't worry, in fact I'd already spoken to your wife about it...

She says:

I'm so sorry.

She says:

Could you pass me a piece of chewing gum from the glove compartment?

He takes the packet out, reads the list of ingredients, reaches the packet towards her to shake one pastille into her hand, and, without looking at her, says:

Irina, my wife, used to say there were so many pre-servatives in what we eat that we're going to have trouble rotting and decomposing when we're dead...

Ah? (With a swift flick of her hand she pops the gum in her mouth.)

Our bodies will politely preserve themselves for months while the maggots wait in despair...

Was she buried?

And it'll change the whole food chain...

Was she buried?

Why? Do you want us to go and see if she's decomposed?

Marie Marie looks horrified. As if she has swallowed a live song thrush.

Don't worry, she was cremated, Lancelot reassures her.

In fact, since bringing the urn home, Lancelot has been torturing himself with this question. Had Irina asked to be cremated or was it an idea of Lancelot's? He remembers discussing it with her, but does not remember the conclusion they reached. Irina told him how she once took the ashes of a close friend somewhere in a taxi, she had far too much drink inside her, given how grief-stricken she was, and absolutely no money, given the life she led then, so she put her dear friend's ashes, which were still warm, into a plastic bag, not an urn, the bag melted in the taxi and the ashes spread all over the rear seat, and she was so heartbroken and so drunk she had no idea what to do, she tried to put them back in the bag but it had holes in it so she quietly panicked in the back of that taxi and ended up spreading the ashes over the floor and the seat as best she could so the driver would not notice anything, then she got out, paid her fare with what money she had left, and, still crying, set off along the pavement with her ragged plastic bag dangling from her hand, she watched the taxi turn at the end of the street and drive away, taking with it her dear friend's ashes scattered over the carpet in the footwell.

Marie Marie is not talking, she seems to be sulking. Her golden earrings shaped like swings in a parrot's cage lurch backwards and forwards, making Lancelot feel seasick; he cannot take his eyes off them, hypnotized.

He presses himself against the door to get as far as he can from her and her reconstituted raspberry smell.

Lancelot tells himself, I've got to get away from this sinister place, I need to get back further south, I can't stand this snow and cold any longer.

He says to himself, I have terrible thoughts.

He says to himself, I only seem to dream about violence and destruction.

Marie Marie stops at a service station. She gets out of the car, and Lancelot throws himself on the file between his legs and opens the client details, he avoids lowering his head so she does not grasp that he is reading. He just orientates his eyes downwards, which affords him a searing migraine pain. He can hear her fiddling about at the back of the car.

Irina lied about her date of birth. She said she was a writer (she wants somewhere quiet with a garden), that her husband was a university professor in comparative literature, that he had a teenage son from a previous relationship and had just inherited a tidy sum.

He becomes aware of a shadow over him, snaps the file shut and pulls his jacket across it, Marie Marie looks at him through the passenger window and gestures to him to open the window. I'm going to get a snack to eat, she says, shall I get you something? He shakes his head, she shrugs and walks off towards the building, slightly hunched, holding her hands away from her body to keep her balance.

Lancelot dives back into the file, straining his eyes wide, Marie Marie's writing is not always legible but she has underlined some words so he can retrace the story Irina gave her.

Irina asked to view very <u>opulent</u> houses. Marie Marie showed her three. But apparently, on seeing the pictures, Irina asked <u>specifically</u> to see Mr <u>Romero</u>'s property. Marie Marie has made a note in the margin: away (business trip Africa, back in two months).

Above she has added in her irregular writing, <u>Smitten</u>. Wants second viewing.

Then in capitals: DECEASED. Contact husband for condolences.

Lancelot closes the file, lays it back down between his feet on the sediment of the carpet, and sees Marie Marie coming back towards him across the tarmac of the service station, she seems tiny and fragile and he is worried she could be run over by a driver taking off without paying.

She opens her door and sits back down, breathing heavily, then starts the car and rejoins the main road, she looks frozen, Lancelot watches her for a moment and asks her whether she would like to have a drink with him to recover from all the emotion, she glances at him, suspiciously, he smiles at her, she shrugs again, If you like, she says.

NINETEEN

They cover a few kilometres in silence and Lancelot eventually notices an illuminated sign shaped like a pagoda flashing mournfully by the roadside. The street lights are coming on along the verge, Lancelot tells Marie Marie to stop in the deserted car park. She does so, poker-faced.

They go into the restaurant and are greeted by a smell of disinfectant combined with the vestiges of over-spiced cooking, in a large room shrouded in near darkness. It must be big enough to accommodate several hundred people, for weddings, seminars and gatherings for sects with gurus clutching microphones and haranguing the crowds with promises of a better future, lower taxes and more self-belief. The place is empty. There is just a huge greenish aquarium with downy weeds and some white fish. Lots of them, albinos, swimming slowly in that morgue-like lighting, docilely carrying on with their melancholy trips back and forth between the extremities of their container which is green with algae.

Lancelot and Marie Marie sit near the door, as if to facilitate a rapid exit in case of an emergency.

A waiter emerges from the back of the room. He does not seem surprised that Lancelot and Marie Marie have turned up, you could be forgiven for thinking it happens every day, two solitary people braving snowstorms and coming to warm themselves in his restaurant. He presents them with the menu with the slow pomp of a butler, Lancelot just asks for a cup of tea and Marie Marie a red Martini. The waiter retreats in silence as if walking on cushions of air. He has not uttered a single word. Lancelot turns to Marie Marie, relieved by her very slightly stubborn expression, she still has a little girl's air of innocence, a sort of steady credulity mixed with celestial stupidity.

I want to find a house my wife would have liked, he begins.

She nods, understandingly, and waits for her drink before launching into describing how much Irina loved the house that has disappeared. She wanted a house with a cellar, she tells him, for their son so he could make 'his' music. Suddenly mentioning him like that, Marie Marie seems to remember this business of a stepson and to feel a bit guilty for not asking for news of the teenager sooner, it gives her a slight shock to think the boy exists, she looks rather panicky as she clings to her glass of red Martini, her eyes cloud over, she asks how the boy is coping with his stepmother's death, and tries to explain that she herself knows a teenager who lost his father and almost went off the rails but eventually enlisted, he went away to the Middle East and came back with malaria and an Israeli girl with an odd name, something like Alona or Aloua, but anyway she couldn't adapt to our harsh climate or the way we ate, she was born in Tel Aviv, so you can imagine, in the end they went back there, to live on a kibbutz, apparently there still are some, crazy isn't it that there still are any, but anyway, Marie Marie ties herself in knots, she cannot work out how to pick up the thread of Lancelot's life again, It's a different story for your son, she says, at least he's got his music. Lancelot, who has no trouble talking about his imaginary son, says that the boy has gone back to be with his mother for a while, she lives in Camerone, she's remarried to a TV salesman, Marie Marie nods, she sees what he means, Lancelot adopts a concerned expression, frowns, lets his shoulders droop visibly and says, Yes yes Irina wanted the boy to have a studio for his rehearsals. Marie Marie nods her head enthusiastically, taking a sip of her Martini, and says, Your wife asked for the plans of the basement to show to your architect, she spent an incredible amount of time in the cellar exploring various options for doing it up. When she seems to have exhausted the subject, Lancelot smiles at her, sits back in his chair and waits for her to polish off her second glass of Martini. He wonders what the combined effects of alcohol and her short-sightedness are going to do to her driving.

Could you drop me at the Central Hotel? he asks. She nods, apparently relieved by this practical question, they get up and go out into the cold, which shrinks your eyelids and attacks your sinuses but does not seem to bother Marie Marie in the least. They set off again in the car. Lancelot wants to speak to Irina's father straight away, he feels the need to see the photos of Irina as a child that the man claims he always has on him, he longs to hear someone talk about his sweetheart again, he wants to go and find this man, then go to the police station to explain the situation, he imagines that if he is more transparent himself, then they will not be so reticent about telling him their findings.

When Marie Marie drops him outside the Central Hotel, smiling at him and screwing up her eyes oddly (as if wanting to hide the intensity of her expression because it contradicts the smile she is putting on), Lancelot – in response to the cold piercing his lungs – thinks once again, Got to get away from here. The light is fading, We're embarking on months of darkness and frost, Lancelot thinks. He runs to the doorway of the hotel and steps into the dry, dusty heat (mites swarm down his trachea), the carpeting looks so old and synthetic Lancelot is amazed he does not produce sparks of static electricity as he walks towards reception, it is November coloured and the walls are painted to match. He asks to see his father-in-law, room twelve. The half-manatee, half-lizard creature filling every corner of space behind the counter opens the register, shakes her head and announces that he left yesterday evening.

Lancelot sighs and says, Obviously.

He leans over the counter to see what name Irina's father used, and there, in the girl's assiduous rounded writing, he sees the name his presumed father-in-law gave in order to have a room: Paco Picasso.

TWENTY

The manatee's colleague, who had just finished her shift, was happy to drop Lancelot outside his house. There were no more buses, no neighbours to call for help, no taxis available for two hours, they felt rather sorry for him, they must have known, the whole world knew in Catano, that he had been married to Irina, that he was a widower and inconsolable, perhaps they knew Irina better than Lancelot did himself, it was even possible that Irina had spent part of every afternoon at the Central Hotel meeting peculiar men with ridiculous names. In any event, he succeeded in getting a lift without making too much fuss. They were understanding and discreet. Perfect.

When the girl drops him outside his house Lancelot waits for her to drive off and gives her a little wave.

He watches the rear lights dwindle.

He says to himself, I need a couple more pills.

And I need to get inside really quickly before I freeze on the spot and go mad. He would give pretty much anything to find Irina inside and live with her in a house with a patio and little streets around it which all lead down to the sea, they would eat grilled fish and peppers in olive oil, he would never ask her any questions and they would live to a hundred and twenty.

Lancelot opens the front door of his house, does not put any lights on, slumps into his armchair and listens to the message flashing red in the dark of the living room. It says to call Detective Schneider back. He checks the time and tries his luck. The detective is in fact still in her office, she answers the telephone and explains straight away what it is about. Irina didn't actually drown but was poisoned with ammonia anhydride. (What's that then?) The results of the analyses have just arrived on her desk. (And why was she cremated before they had the results? Wasn't that a bit negligent? I'm not sure I'm not going to take you to court, Detective Schneider.) Ammonia anhydride acts slowly, the victim is administered (or administers themself) small daily doses of poison over several months without any cause for suspicion. There are no visible effects until the maximum dose the body can absorb is reached. Only then does the heart pack in. It's like a little cardiac implosion. And bang, no one left, Detective Schneider says with her customary tact. Lancelot murmurs, Yes, yes, of course. He tells himself the detective definitely underestimates him. She adds, It's a bit like pananoval. He mumbles that he has no idea what she is talking about. The detective sighs as if tired of having to give explanations. She is always particularly keen for whoever she is addressing to gauge the full extent of her knowledge and patience. So she clarifies, It's a poison they used to give to political prisoners in Argentina in the heyday of the dictatorship. Impossible to detect. The guys they wanted to get rid of slipped into unconsciousness and, just before the final heart attack, they were chucked into the water. They drowned. She gives a little cough. Clever and unstoppable, she concludes.

And out of the blue she asks him, Do you know a Kurt Bayer?

Lancelot then feels terribly weary, he can tell what she is going to reveal to him, he would just like to sit down and go to sleep in his chair, and instead of answering her question about this Kurt Bayer, he asks Detective Schneider why Irina is dead and whether she suspects him, Lancelot, of killing her. Detective Schneider hesitates, seems to chew on something then retorts, You haven't answered my question, Mr Rubinstein. So Lancelot sighs and asks, Who's Kurt Bayer? Detective Schneider resumes her usual tone, slightly brusque like a primary-school teacher afraid of being sweet-talked, and says, He's the owner of the car your wife was found in. Then without drawing breath, and this is a woman whose breath whistles because her lungs can hardly cope any more from being squashed between her other bloated organs, she adds, Could you come to my office first thing tomorrow morning? I'd like to go over a few points with you. Lancelot shakes his head, alone in the dark of his living room, standing next to the pedestal table with the telephone and the heart-shaped block of pink paper Irina used for messages. What sort of points? he asks. Things to do with your wife's work, replies the detective. Mmm, mmm, Lancelot manages. All right, I'll come over tomorrow morning. And he hangs up gently. Tomorrow the detective will ask him questions he will be unable to answer. At the end of the day, they know about as much as each other. He stays there for a moment a little dazed to think he has told no one of Irina's death (and he has no one to tell), and the only way he could get numbers for her work contacts and even the people she was supposedly joining when catching the plane that ill-fated evening would be from her mobile (which came to the end of its mobile life in the icy waters under the Omoko bridge). And there he is, Lancelot, dumbstruck by how little he knew her. He tells himself that what is worrying about Doctor Epstein's blue capsules is they are meant to distance him from reckless suicidal impulses (black thoughts, as Doctor Epstein euphemistically calls them), when in fact they put him in a state of only moderate despair which might lead him to weigh up sensibly the pros and cons between a gun with rusty bullets which would cause infection, and a good length of mountaineering rope tied to the curtain rail. Lancelot tells himself he is complicating things. The blue capsules – which are supposed to spare him – give him a feeling of total calm which makes him want to die. They produce a tremendous longing not to exist. Lancelot considers this and realizes they are as relaxing and dangerous as a scalding hot bath taken in the dark.

TWENTY-ONE

When Lancelot was a child his mother used to tell him that his father had a wife (A shrew) and a little girl two years older than him (Cynthia). She told him that one day he could claim his rights as this man's son, that there was a three-hundred-square-metre apartment that was partly his, as was half the pair of Arab horses in livery at a stud a few hundred kilometres from the apartment in question, she added that he could help himself to the powerboat (It's not a girl's sport) and that he need only supply a DNA profile, which is standard procedure for illegitimate princes and princesses, and the truth could blow up in everyone's face.

With these words she would spread her arms and roll her eyes, and Lancelot felt he could see an error message pop up, with its characteristic warning chime, saying, You have unexpectedly exited the programme. Please contact your dealer if the problem persists.

She would be sprawled on the sofa, looking around as if waking from a long deep sleep and suddenly discovering the shocking state of that sofa and carpet.

As a result of this tale, Lancelot, who secretly liked photostories and tear-jerking Spanish films, imagined when he met Irina that she could very easily have been his sister. He felt so close to her that he gave in to what had been his adolescent failings, his yearning for fusion, we're friends for life, we said the same thing at the same time, it's a sign, you're my chosen sister, my chosen brother, let's set off on an adventure.

Deep down, the only way he managed to formulate his love for Irina was in these terms: If I had been a woman, I would have liked to be like her. Which, all in all, is a pretty dubious way of seeing things.

He fairly soon realized that this scenario of his did not hold any water, the few times she mentioned her parents, the tacky cocoon she had emerged from bore no relation to Lancelot's father's family, its boredom-riddled escapades and garden parties.

Lancelot knew that he was very specifically drawn to poor little unhappy girls whose childhood lay in tatters, and that this was something to do with his own mother. A form of determinism that left him feeling completely helpless. He thought, I'm drawn to pretty girls who are broken inside. And he felt a mixture of pride and disgust which knocked the breath out of him – like when you save someone from drowning and then steal their wallet as you haul them onto the shore.

He had little information about Irina's childhood, she only talked about her mother, they had supper together in the kitchen every evening much earlier than her father, who came home late from his building sites. The mother wore her hair in a chignon and put a scarf over the top, knotting it under her chin as if she were Audrey Hepburn in an open-top car, it conferred a certain handsome washer-woman dignity on her because of the hand-knitted lacy cardigans she wore with her polka-dot scarves. She made Irina wear knitted dresses against her skin, which produced bouts of eczema in the folds of her body (as an adult the very sight of a knitted dress could still make a smattering of tiny white spots spring up on Irina's fingers, they itched so dreadfully she ended up tearing her skin off with her nails). Her mother forbade her from looking inside cafés – she would administer little smacks to the back of her head when they walked past the window of a bistro to make Irina keep up the same pace and not slither her gaze into those dens of iniquity.

And the more he thinks about it, the more Lancelot is struck by the paucity of information he managed to glean about his beloved. If and when he did try to question her in the early days of their relationship, she would evade the issue and frown as if accusing him of wanting to throw a fit of jealousy after the event. He eventually silenced his own inquisitorial enthusiasm so as not to frighten off or hurt his sweetheart. With the net result that all he knew about her was the feel of her skin, her weakness for strong spirits and her love of animals facing extinction.

Lancelot takes a sports bag and fills it with warm clothes and skin-repair creams containing aloe vera (Irina seemed to fill whole shelves of the medicine cabinet with the things). When the bag gets too heavy to carry, Lancelot stands there gazing at the contents spewing from the opening, he frowns and tugs on the zip like a madman until it peels open irreparably, Lancelot swears between clenched teeth, Fuckfuckfuck, goes off to get some tape, comes back with a white roll marked two hundred thousand times with the word FRAGILE in red (a vestige of their move to this house of happiness), and mummifies his sports bag, doggedly working his way through the tape until the roll is completely finished.

He kicks it down the staircase and the bag tumbles down a few stairs then stops, Lancelot follows it, clinging to the banister and furiously kicking the bag so that it lands on the ground floor, then he drags it to the garage and rams it into the boot of the car with tremendous effort, as if the bag holds something far heavier and more alive than it actually does. Lancelot goes back upstairs to find his papers, his money, his mobile, which is no use to him at all but he cannot imagine leaving it there, the blue pills and some pictures of Irina (smiling, with teeth and hair and blood pumping through her veins), he wisely omits the urn containing Irina's ashes and microscopic bits of bone which belong as much to Irina as to the previous occupant of the oven in which her body was burned, goes back to the car, puts *Norma* on at full volume on the car radio, then goes and switches off all the lights and locks up the house as if leaving on a very long journey.

PART THREE

TWENTY-TWO

Irina liked children in a very unusual way.

For a start she never wanted any.

She talked about it with Lancelot in the early days of their relationship, putting forward fairly discouraging arguments about the state of the world and water shortages. She had expounded at length on the reasons stopping her procreating; these were related to the extinction of the pangolin, the new threat of fascism, and pollution in the water table. Lancelot, who had no particular urge to reproduce, but, had he done, would have liked it to be with her, listened attentively, he felt understanding but was slightly disappointed – he wanted to screw this rag of disappointment into a tight little ball, and was sure he could throw it far away from himself so he no longer thought about it. What seemed most important at the time was having the privilege of waking every morning beside this beautiful woman, something which never ceased to delight him – he would open one eye and immediately start smiling,

129

Oh, yes, that's right, he would say to himself, I'm with Irina, he touched her skin and sighed contentedly, his happiness like a star nestled in his chest, beneath his ribcage, radiating a pale warmth.

When they moved to Catano Lancelot and Irina had neighbours, a man who bred pointers and lived with his six-year-old daughter in a small house just three hundred metres away.

The child's name was Tralala. That was how she introduced herself to Irina and Lancelot when they first met her. Irina found the nickname very jolly but also very sad. She often swung between two extremes, readily deeming things depressing as well as thrilling. And when Lancelot asked why she thought Tralala was sad and jolly she said, I think it's very pretty (and she waggled her head like a puppet to show that the name reminded her of pealing bells), but it's also the name of a transsexual prostitute who dies alone on a stretch of wasteland in one of Selby's books.

Tralala often came to see them, singing to herself as she walked along the road and lurched down the slope to their house, accompanied by one of her father's pointers.

She knocked on the door and cried, Knock knock knock, very loudly. When Irina opened the door, she would come in and the dog would lie down on the veranda with its head between its paws, blinking slowly and furrowing its brow into a melancholy frown. It acted as a bodyguard, not getting involved in the client's private life, all that was missing were the earpiece and the three-piece suit hiding a bullet-proof vest.

Tralala would turn to the animal and say, I'll be back, Darling. She called all her father's dogs Darling, and if anyone asked her whether she liked dogs in general she would say, Yes, specially the colour (because in her brief life she had met very few dogs other than her father's pointers).

If Irina and Lancelot were too busy to pay her any attention, they offered her a Tex Avery cartoon and she would say, Yes, yes, a texavery, as if it were the name of a strawberry fruit drink. She ran over to the sofa and slumped onto it with a sigh, I'm exhausted with tiredness, then, remote control in hand, she made slow-motion sequences of scenes where the stunning redhead sways her hips and drives the wolf wild. Tralala called her The Pretty Lady, she said, I love the bits with The Pretty Lady, and she pressed PLAY, then PAUSE, then PLAY, then PAUSE, and loved capturing her and immobilizing her every time she made a move.

One day she said to Lancelot, She looks like my mummy, and Lancelot nodded, thinking, Of course of course (then one time he went to Tralala's house and there was a picture of her mother on the sideboard, and she really did have orange hair, a round mouth and eyeliner a good half a centimetre thick emphasizing her eyes).

Tralala did not have a mother, she had died of cancer two years earlier. Tralala used to say, I no longer believe in God, otherwise why would he have done this to me? If someone ever told her her mother had become a star in the firmament, she shrugged her shoulders and shook her head. I don't believe in all that, she announced. And it was more like a settling of scores with God (if I upset him he might show up) than a true declaration of scepticism.

Lancelot once told Irina:

I like seeing you with Tralala.

Without looking up she retorted:

I can see you coming.

Then she turned to face him, put both fists on her hips and said:

She actually bears out my theory that there's no point making more children when there are already so many who need looking after.

I know, he conceded.

And are you so proud of your genetic resources that you consider it indispensable to reproduce them?

Lancelot frowned but abandoned the discussion, he just said, Sorry, and she replied, Sorry.

Irina had long rambling conversations with Tralala, she showed her the documentaries she made (whale sharks in the coral reefs off Belize and how they were proliferating because the water temperature was rising), they would sit down on the sofa, Tralala settling her head on Irina's shoulder and taking one of her arms to put it round her own neck, then she would suck her fingers and stop moving altogether, barely breathing, so still she could easily have been mistaken for a cushion.

Tralala spent a lot of time in front of the television, which had a very particular effect on the way she saw things, she drew figures in two dimensions as if they had been slapped onto the paper and she surrounded them with a black frame. Sometimes she even drew little circles on the right-hand side of the paper – the volume and contrast buttons.

Tralala talked to her own hands and hardly ever went to school. When Tralala's mother was dying she taught her to read, and the father could not see what the child would gain from some academic establishment – It wouldn't do you any good, anyway, it's a slackers' factory, he kept saying. And every time Lancelot heard him making this sort of pronouncement, he would think, That can't be right, he can't honestly believe that stuff.

When Lancelot came home from shopping he regularly found Tralala and Irina dancing in the living room with their hair all messed up, holding hands, throwing their heads around and swinging their bottoms, with the stereo on maximum volume. Lancelot stayed on the doorstep, they did not hear him come in but carried on watching each other as they wiggled about with shining eyes and pink cheeks, they seemed afraid of losing sight of each other. Tralala moved oddly, as if she were underwater or imagined she was the most graceful person on earth, describing great arabesques with her arms and tottering about, knocking over smaller pieces of furniture. Lancelot would beat a retreat, he had always had trouble with rock and roll, electric guitars meant nothing to him, they made him feel the foundations of the house had come unstuck, he could almost feel the ground giving way beneath his feet, so he went back out, sat on the veranda with his plastic bags full of food, and waited for the commotion to die down. He gazed into the distance, not really noticing how cold it was. He was slightly anaesthetized. This is nice, he told himself, it's really very nice. When the noise stopped he went back into the house, they had collapsed on the sofa and honestly looked as excited as children given tickets for the fair, they watched him come in as if he were returning from some distant island and they had made a life together while he was away, they would smile and burst out laughing, and Lancelot loved seeing them like that.

When Irina went away on location, Tralala still came over, sometimes with her father. The latter would bring beer and peanuts, as if he thought Lancelot incapable of keeping any in his own cupboards. He talked about his dogs and Tralala's mother. And Tralala sat on the floor right next to them, playing with her hands, ashen as a consumptive waif, creating a huge variety of geometric shapes with her fingers and accompanying her usual singing with a funny sound in her throat, something that made her vocal cords vibrate, you could hear the vibration clearly, you could picture her rigid vocal cords quivering as she went on and on singing the same dismal, repetitive tune. Sometimes she got up, went and found the Scrabble set in the room at the back and sat down on the tiled floor of the kitchen near the fridge. She lined the letters up on the floor to make words. She never tidied the letters away into the box when she and her father left. Then, when they were gone, Lancelot would go straight to the kitchen, impatient to read the secret message she had left him, and he would contemplate the sentences Tralala had written: I'm hungry and throbbing; hush my skin; naked and light for you; another feline silence. He would stand there, cup of tea in hand, facing the purring fridge, believing he could understand something of the child. He started breathing very slowly and thought he could then shed light on some mystery.

And then Tralala disappeared.

She did not come over for several days so Lancelot called the child's father.

Hello, it's Lancelot, I hope I'm not disturbing you?

Lancelot?

He sounded so surprised that Lancelot gave his surname too.

Er… is everything all right?

No.

What's going on?

I'm all alone. Tralala's gone.

Lancelot felt a great surge, not just of acid panic which immobilized his organs, but also of images of a child found in a ditch with her skirts up around her midriff. He swallowed hard.

When.

Three days ago?

That's beginning to be a hell of a long time.

S'pose so.

Have you arranged any searches?

Searches?

Yes, to find her.

Find her? But I know where she is.

Lancelot started hyperventilating, producing a breathless sound like a spaniel after chasing a partridge, not realizing the battle was lost in advance – wings versus legs.

I don't really understand, he eventually whispered.

She's gone to my sister's.

What's she gone to your sister for?

They're going to put her in the local school in September.

Where is it?

Five hundred from here.

Five hundred what?

Five hundred kilometres.

And in a thick voice Tralala's father explained how his sister and her husband had come over to pick up the child, they had asked Tralala if she would like to go with them and she had said yes.

They've got an eight-year-old boy, he added.

He announced this as if discovering the name of his wife's lover, how pretty the man's bank account looked, and the length of his tool. He tried to explain to Lancelot how his sister and brother-in-law had decreed that Tralala could not go on sleeping in a cardboard box, that, in their house, she would have her own room and a bed, that she would play with dolls, not wild animals like the ones her father bred, someone had to take care of the child's well-being, the sister and her husband asserted, Tralala's father sniggered, saying the girl would set up a cardboard box in the middle of her room again, a big box with cushions and blankets, that she would make it her den, and the two dickheads wouldn't be able to do anything about it, they could try as hard as they liked to make her sleep in a pink bed full of frills, the child would set herself up as she always did, she would draw windows on her box with a marker pen and go on a sleeping strike if forced to leave her den, she knew how to do that sort of thing, sitting cross-legged, stiff as a post against her pillows, eyes wide open and not blinking, a trick she had perfected, a trick you couldn't help admiring, or she would clink the metal upright of her bed with a teaspoon all night, she would drive them mad, and then they would bring his little girl home to him and stop threatening to send her to social services.

Have you been drinking? Lancelot asked.

That's not the point.

I know, but have you been drinking?

Tralala's father hung up without another word.

When Lancelot told her, Irina decided to go and see for herself what was going on in Tralala's household.

I'll come with you, said Lancelot.

Out of the question.

Why? (Lancelot, arms dangling limply, eyebrows raised, No one wants me, everyone hates me, everyone rejects me.)

You know perfectly well he'll trust me more.

No, I didn't know.

Come on, my big boy, he's going to want to pour his heart out and he won't want you to see him in that state.

Lancelot turned his back and grumbled:

All right.

When Irina left the house it was ten o'clock in the morning, she came back nine hours later.

What did you do all that time? asked Lancelot, who had spent the whole day resisting the urge to call on some fallacious pretext, and fighting the impulse to go snooping casually under Tralala's father's windows.

We talked.

Is that all?

No, I forgot. We fucked like savages.

That's clever.

Oh, my poor love's lost his sense of humour.

It's not funny.

Sorry.

Sorry.

Irina flopped down on the sofa, reached her hand towards the bar and gave Lancelot an exhausted smile to get him to fix her a pick-me-up. He went to the kitchen to find some tonic water while, still on the sofa, she relayed what information she had gathered. She bellowed it out so he missed nothing. She shouted that the father's sister really had taken the little girl. And she was a Mennonite too.

A Mennonite? said Lancelot, coming back into the living room with a tray.

Yes, you know, those people who don't know what a TV is, who drive around in carts (here Lancelot pictured the sister in a black smock, taking Tralala away in a horse-drawn trap and driving through Catano, sitting bolt upright with her headdress perfectly straight), their children all get jaundice because they're so interbred, they don't drink any alcohol, they think rock and roll comes straight from hell to lead their souls astray, and they won't have anything made of plastic in their homes.

But how did they succeed in taking the child?

Tralala's father has already had a brush with the law.

(A brush with? Lancelot wondered where this expression came from. He dwelt on it, picked it apart, thought of a broom sweeping briskly, the pile of dust and fluff building into an airy, downy mountain, he let the dust pile waft right across the room, then came back to his senses.)

I didn't know that.

You didn't know what?

That he'd had trouble with the law.

But I was just saying how he left for Camerone...

I'm sorry.

You're not listening to me.

I am. But I'm a bit shaken up by the whole thing, I didn't really follow...

You're not listening to me.

I am, I tell you.

All right. (She affected a pause so that Lancelot could gauge her clemency, and fully appreciate the rest of the story.) As I was saying, she went on, he's in complete despair and just can't imagine staying here on his own. I tried to persuade him not to go. I think the decision's too hasty. But there was nothing for it. He's off to live in Camerone, he's selling the dogs and he's going to be an escalator repairman.

What are you talking about?

Apparently it's his first job...

First.

Besides breeding pointers.

What a load of... said Lancelot, shaking his head.

I don't know what to think.

And who's he going to sell his dogs to?

I don't know. Maybe we could have one.

No.

No?

It wouldn't be possible. You're always off all over the place. And, you know, me and dogs, I just can't.

Let's stop talking about it.

Sorry.

Sorry.

And Tralala's father left their little house three hundred metres from Lancelot and Irina's, he barricaded it up as if it were mined, nailing planks to the windows and painting skulls and crossbones over the façade to dissuade local kids from meddling. Then he piled his things in his old Toyota, came and kissed Irina and shook Lancelot's paw (he smelt of beer, old beer depositing a sediment in his organs, sploshing about in the bottom of his stomach since forever, this was at half past seven in the morning), he gave Tralala's address to Irina (and throughout the time she had left to live Irina wrote to the child without ever receiving a reply), then he left in his car, which made a clattering sound like metal implements shaken up in a canvas bag, and with a wave of his hand he eclipsed himself to turn into an escalator repairman. Irina cried. She had lost Tralala. And Tralala's father.

She cried right through till evening.

Tralala's father was called Kurt Bayer.

He was the man who owned the car (which was not actually a clapped-out Toyota) in which Irina ended her days at the bottom of the Omoko's frozen waters.

His name was Kurt Bayer and Lancelot cannot stop thinking about him as he speeds towards Camerone through the snow, wanting to get away from the shingle-roofed house he shared with Irina as quickly as he can, the place now feels evil to him (he would give anything for a pyromaniac child to go and reduce the place to ashes), he even goes so far as to imagine it was built over an old Indian cemetery (there are no Indians in the area), or a Neanderthal one, then (did they bury their dead?).

TWENTY-THREE

Lancelot stops at the first service station he finds on his way. He thinks he will be brutally frozen the instant he opens the door (with a sharp, deafening snap like the noise produced by successive layers of ice forming over the lake, each cracking sound can be heard several kilometres away and then people know the winter is taking a turn for the worse), he twists round to the rear seat to tell his imaginary children he won't be long, rummages in the glove compartment for his money and stumbles across some relics of Irina. That is what he says to himself, These are relics of Irina. And he thinks of the Holy Shroud.

Irina's relics are:

two tubes of Redder Than Red lipstick (one almost finished, the other barely started);

three airline teaspoons (like everyone else, Irina nicked these teaspoons, her favourites were Swiss Air ones, sometimes she was prepared to go to India via Zurich just so she could steal the teaspoon from her tinned fruit salad);

ten stable iodine tablets (obviously to counter radio-active iodine in case of a nuclear incident or dirty bomb);

a perfume vaporizer (rose-scented, Irina used to say that the smell of wisteria, freesia, lilac and lily of the valley could not be extracted from the flower but only chemically reconstituted. And Irina loathed chemical reconstitutions. At least she claimed she did);

a torch;

a green plastic bracelet which separates into two identical parts so that it can be put on, and then fuses round the wrist thanks to the magnets inside it;

a page from a magazine folded in four, one side refers to cornflakes coated in organic chocolate (with a discount voucher to cut out) and on the other there is an article about Mosquitone, a sound only teenagers can hear. Lancelot skims through the article, he did not know there was such a thing, he thinks to himself, I'm far too old to hear it, but he wants to test it out, to check he isn't the exception to the rule, then he looks at the discount voucher and wonders which side of the page Irina was interested in.

When he has filled the tank he sets off again, trying to disconnect his brain from the thoughts preoccupying him, striving to concentrate only on the road and the distance between street lights. Heavy lorries overtaking him boom like steamboats and create such an in-draught that Lancelot clings to his steering wheel and stops breathing for a few seconds as the lorries swish past.

His mobile rings, he glances at the number on the screen, it is the estate agent's, he waits for the caller to leave a message and presses the speaker button so he can listen to it as he drives along.

It is Marie Marie asking, in a tiny little voice, whether he would like to view any other houses, whether he needs to talk, whether he's got a couple of minutes, she gives a little cough and wishes him a pleasant day, he listens to the message again, her voice is fluty and melodious, there is nothing pink or brash about it. He is touched that she should call. It is a long time since he has received calls from anyone but Detective Schneider. He saves the message. So he can listen to it again at his leisure. Then tries to concentrate on the road again.

But his mind keeps coming back to the fact that the only person he knows in Camerone – apart from Kurt Bayer, and Lancelot suspects finding him would be no mean feat – and the only person who might just remember him is Elisabeth, his first wife. A thought that leaves him wide-eyed with horror, prepared to launch his car and everything inside it (himself, his sad memories, those fucking stable iodine tablets which are just another sign of how crazy Irina was, the lipsticks which would explode into particles of matt red paint, and the teaspoons she stole at the cost of thousands of litres of aviation fuel) against the crash barrier which, despite its name, is specifically intended to prevent crashes, he is quite ready to hurtle into its metallic horizontalness, can already see himself doing it, giving the fatal swing of the steering wheel, he can picture the car waltzing through the air, smoking and coming to rest on its roof like a great handicapped tortoise, the wheels still spinning, the carcass clicking and losing its fluids and eventually exploding in several places at once and burning Lancelot and everything inside it (and then, yes, I'd be well on my way with my stable iodine tablets).

The other parasitic thought is the impression that he is running away both from a booby-trapped, haunted place (the house) and from perverse, pointed interrogations (à la Detective Schneider).

Running away makes him look suspect.

But when all is said and done, only a bit more or a bit less.

He says to himself, I can never move until I'm cornered.

The option of bringing an end to it all (skidding into the let's-really-crash barrier or overdosing on Doctor Epstein's blue pills) makes the situation less trying. It reminds him of his despair as a child, his despair at being the son of a woman constantly abandoned by the men she loved – he was convinced he would have to take care of her till kingdom come, even when she was lost in the depths of some caravan, suffering from incontinence and chronic intestinal obstructions, that it was the cross he had to bear and his duty and his own fault and the solution available to him, if he wanted to avoid this purgatory, was to finish with it straight away (or maybe tomorrow) by slitting his wrists with a Stanley knife in the bathroom basin.

Lancelot was a fairly morose little boy.

But his mother spared him this sort of complication by dying of septicaemia following the extraction of a wisdom tooth.

Lancelot was sixteen at the time.

And he felt sad, lonely and relieved.

He went and lived in a home for the time he still had to do before coming of age. Then he turned himself into a student, a serious, boring, grant-funded student. And he met Elisabeth on the steps of the university library.

Lancelot tries to concentrate on the road again. He switches on the radio to hear the world go by. He watches cars overtake him, turning his head to see the drivers' faces. It's always very strange, that illusion of speed and im-mobility when a car overtakes and you get a silent glimpse of the driver's expression. You eye each other up and both cross the Styx in silence. That is when Lancelot recognizes, or thinks he recognizes, the face of the driver in the grey car overtaking him on the right. Their eyes meet both furtively and slowly, as if suspended in time. It is the tall Paco Picasso, Irina's resuscitated father. Lancelot blinks, he swerves slightly, producing a surge of adrenaline in him which electrifies his arms. He leans forwards and studies the car that has overtaken him. It is not grey but blue. It continues on its way. Lancelot would like to have the luxury of panicking, but this is not the right place, he is pretty sure of that. He opens his eyes wide, gradually regains his calm, feels his heartbeat slow after its little dance, and focuses on the white lines filing past hypnotically and disappearing as if the car were swallowing them one after the other.

TWENTY-FOUR

Irina's absence is as impressive as her presence. Her absence seems to have stamped out the exact volume of air in the exact same shape as her presence. You could feel you were sitting beside Irina's absence. It is a completely plausible concept.

TWENTY-FIVE

Lancelot rested only once along the way, he slept in his car at a motorway stop, thinking he might be turfed out of the place by someone wielding a cudgel, or held up at gunpoint. He wakes to a cardboard mouth and a stiff neck in among the HGVs snoring with their curtains drawn in the car park. He feels like a torpedo fish in a school of killer whales. He sets off again.

He stops at a service station every three hours, wandering round the aisles listening to 'Eine Kleine Nachtmusik', and thinking, Everything here is orderly luxurious calm and pleasurable, he says to himself, I could live just in places like this, I'd like to stay here for ever. Then he buys some carpaccio-flavoured crisps and later some chestnut-flavoured chewing gum; he does not read the ingredients, to piss Irina off, and spends some time with the lucky-dip machines. He puts a coin in the slot and is rewarded with a Super Tortoise from Dragon Ball, he opens the capsule containing the character but has no idea who

Super Tortoise is, so he leaves the toy in an obvious place on the outside windowsill, for a child to take.

He goes back to his car.

He looks at the rear seat.

But there is no one in the rear seat. Nor in the passenger seat for that matter.

Lancelot eats his carpaccio-flavoured crisps, then takes four chewing gums and decides to swallow them.

And he continues on his way.

He goes back to his obsessive mummy-Irina comparison. It keeps him busy. He feels he can tick off the points. It is like organizing a bout of mud-wrestling.

He realizes that both of them tended to make preparations for surviving disasters – an air attack, a hurricane devastating the town and its communications networks, a power cut lasting several weeks (some sugar, some sugar, if I've only got one kilo of sugar then I haven't really got any), a hike in fuel prices, Lancelot's mother stocking up on packets of Chinese noodles and tins of sweetcorn and tuna chunks at the slightest price rise, Irina's fears about talks between the United States and North Korea, the information she gathered about Minamata disease and accounts from Chernobyl survivors, the terror that sometimes gripped her and made her put on a great oiled sou'wester the minute it rained, practically strangling herself as she did up her hood, for fear of being affected by acid rain. Lancelot remembers Irina's defiance about pesticides, a defiance she nourished by losing herself in medico-spiritual reviews detailing the ravages of extensive agriculture and genetic research, she was captivated by them and kept saying, They're mad, they're completely mad. Which made Lancelot smile. He called this tendency The Great Conspiracy Mania. Irina had a tendency to mention some dangerous, all-powerful Instrument Landing System to encapsulate her fears, and this was also one of Lancelot's mother's symptoms. Except that his mother had long ago focused her indignation on the decadent rich who exploited destitute foreigners. At the end of her life, Lancelot's mother found her distress turning to bitterness: the impoverished foreigners who had been exploited for so long had actually come and stolen her job – she had always been a waitress in a twenty-four-hour restaurant.

Lancelot thinks. He underestimated Irina's guru-searching inclinations. He admits that he saw this foible almost as a physiological trait peculiar to women. He thought it as inevitable and harmless as menstruation.

He could weep about it now.

Lancelot arrives in Camerone the next afternoon.

He tracks down a bed and breakfast in the town centre. It looks out onto a small tree-lined square with an A-frame of Scandinavian swings and a fire station on the left-hand side, he stands by the bedroom window and cannot get over the fact that he is back here. It is a beautiful day. He does not feel tired, even though he has driven for two days and two nights, and rested for only a few hours. He feels a sense of calm, like when you have had so little to eat that the sensation of hunger vanishes, giving way to a great emptiness, the body then feels hollow, and you almost think you could give up food for ever.

Leaning his elbows on the balustrade, he catches sight of two children playing, they have found a frog next to the tiny pond stagnating with duckweed in the middle of the square, they are imitating the frog's leaping, and chasing it under the acacia trees, croaking. Their mother must be sitting on a bench nearby. Lancelot can hear her laughing on the phone. He thinks of the last time he came across a frog, it was last summer in the garden, it was dark and he was with Irina on the veranda, she was drinking her evening gin and he an iced tea, they were watching the stars glimmering, and he hoped she would not mention those stars which have been dead for thousands of years but whose light still reaches us. If she had allowed herself to comment on them it would have distressed him terribly. But Irina said, Oh, something just moved over by the fir tree, Lancelot leant forward to pick up his torch and pointed it into the bushes, he got up and went over, then told Irina, It's a frog, and she started squealing, Don't go near it, don't go near it, don't go near it, I read something about poisonous toads, they don't know how to cope with the things in Australia now, they've already killed ten thousand people. The frog scuttled away. And Lancelot went back over to Irina, with the torch hanging limply in his hand. They stayed like that, motionless, looking at each other sadly, overwhelmed by Irina's outburst, neither of them knowing how to get out of this awkward corner, Lancelot could have laughed or bounced back with a witty retort but he no longer had the strength. He said, It was just a tree frog, a tiny little tree frog. So Irina got up without a word, opened the mosquito screen and went into the house. By watching the lights go on and off, he was able to follow her progress as far as the bathroom and their bedroom, Lancelot sat down again on the veranda, rocked on the rear legs of his chair and, shining the torch back and forth across the garden, studied the definitive darkness beyond its beam.

Remembering that summer evening is quite painful for Lancelot. He leans on his balcony as if every muscle in his neck were tormenting him, and wisely starts watching the firemen cleaning their engine. They seem to want to make it gleam like in a children's book.

A man crosses the street and goes through the gate into the square. He is long and thin as a piece of kindling wood. Lancelot instantly recognizes the clipped stride of a former soldier. He jumps back into the room, sheltered under the awning. He asks himself, What the hell's he doing here? Is he following me?

The man walks under the acacia and sits on the bench. He has a newspaper in his pocket, he unfolds it and Lancelot watches him from above at his leisure.

Is it him or is it not?

Lancelot stiffens. He tells himself, I'm going mad, every thin, uptight man in town isn't Irina's false father, he makes himself close the window and sit down on the side of the bed to call directory enquiries. He asks for Kurt Bayer's number, but the mousy-voiced girl who answers – and probably lives the other side of the country because she asks to have Camerone spelt out – says, I'm sorry, there's no one of that name listed there. So he hangs up and calls reception to ask for a business directory. When he gets it he settles down on the bed, turns on the television, which is attached high up in a corner of the room like a video camera, hits the mute button and launches into the list of escalator repairmen in Camerone. Very soon he comes across Tralala Fixitall – lifts, hoists, all brands of mechanical stairs. Lancelot writes down the number and address. Then goes out and prepares to walk there.

The ramrod-straight man is no longer sitting on the bench in the square. Lancelot nods his head. He is very pleased with himself. For not going out to lie in ambush in the magnolias and check who the man was. Lancelot smiles. He believes he is convalescing and embarking on altogether new paths.

It is warm, the evening is closing in, Lancelot stops and smells the air, he feels like crying out, Whatever did we think we were doing going off to that freezing place where it's dark the whole time? Lancelot looks around as if waking from a long sleep, heaving himself from his glass coffin, Hey what,

what is it? He walks carefully, he has not used his legs for a good while, No, but seriously, just remind me, why did we go poking round that dump all that way away? Eventually he walks past his old apartment – where he lived with Elisabeth before he left her. He looks up and, it's OK, he doesn't pass out, he thinks he sees a figure (is it her?) slip past the living-room window, but he knows full well that he is indulgently deluding himself, he continues on his way, taking great care not to walk on the cracks between the paving stones, he takes one of Doctor Epstein's pills, without any water, so he tries to salivate, the pill sticks in his throat for a few seconds, Lancelot panics for a moment, he can already see himself dying of suffocation and dehydration from the gelatine in the capsule, which will cling to his trachea like a stamp and would rip the wall of his gullet if it were pulled away. He manages to get it down thanks to a succession of idiotic contortions and grimaces in the middle of the pavement right outside his old apartment. The pill is absorbed into the depths of his entrails but for several hours to come Lancelot will still have the unpleasant sensation of it stuck in his throat.

He walks through a leafy square and realizes that what he has missed most are the trees in Camerone, there are cypresses here tapering vertically to unreasonable heights, there are hackberry trees and fig trees, there are acacias and nameless thorny bushes which produce poisonous crimson flowers.

Lancelot walks on and savours the pleasure of being back in Camerone.

He crosses a substantial part of the town in cautious, measured steps.

In the end he stops outside Tralala Fixitall's door.

There are fluorescent plastic letters and logos of spare parts stuck to the window. The place looks closed. Lancelot flattens his nose on the window to look inside. He makes out an old computer on a wooden desk salvaged from a school clear-out, a map of the town on the wall, an originally beige telephone coloured red with a marker pen, a red Chinese lantern hanging from the ceiling, about a hundred and fifty packets (empty ones?) of Craven cigarettes piled into a skyscraper in one corner of the room, a chair on chunky wheels and covered in red acrylic fur behind the desk, and grimacing red and gold dragons taped to the computer; these date back to the Chinese New Year and shine softly in the gloom. Lancelot looks at his watch and then the times written on the door beneath a mobile number. The premises closed an hour ago.

He thinks, Not brilliant brilliant.

He stays there a moment as if thinking, and breathes in the evening air with its lovely smell of dust and diesel.

Lancelot decides to sit in the bar over the road and watch the door to the shop. He feels like James Bond. It is not unpleasant. Like when he was eight and played secret agents with his mother – for want of anyone of a more appropriate age. They would put on mackintoshes and sit at the folding table in the kitchen eating ham and affecting conspiratorial expressions. Lancelot cannot explain why, but every time he thinks about this game he remember the macs and the ham.

He finds a place by the window and sits looking at a beer, he knows he will not drink it but he did not manage to ask for a cup of tea. He waits for twenty minutes, peering so intently at the red shopfront that it leaves a green shadow on his retina when he looks away. A car pulls up, Kurt Bayer gets out of it, looks for his keys, then goes into his office. Lancelot is so stunned by what he has seen that he cannot make up his mind whether to get up and cross the street to talk to the man, or to call Detective Schneider and tell her about his discovery.

He stays there, sitting in front of his untouched beer, his arms hanging limply and his jaw sagging slightly.

Kurt Bayer comes back out, closes the door and, before Lancelot has time to make a move, crosses the street and comes into the bar.

TWENTY-SIX

Kurt Bayer has not seen Lancelot.

He came and sat at the bar, the waitress said, Hello, Klaus, did not ask him what he wanted but poured him a pint and slid it along the counter to him. Kurt Bayer has lost weight. He has lost weight in the way alcoholics sometimes do, his blond head waggles on his neck, almost like the head of an Indian doll on its terracotta base, his hair is long and dirty, he is wearing sunglasses pushed up as a hairband, tired Italian brogues and a khaki-coloured suit in fine corduroy. He has a slight limp and looks like an old surfer who had a bite taken out of his leg by the local great white shark and can find nothing better to do than drift about by the water's edge sipping cans of beer and coming on strong to pretty girls.

Lancelot is perplexed. He wonders what has become of Tralala. And what Irina was still cooking up with this man. And whether Kurt is really called Kurt or Klaus. Or Philemon or Rocco.

Lancelot feels very sad and lonely. He would like to leave

the bar without the other man seeing him, nothing else means anything to him. He says to himself, What if I flatten myself against the window, no one would see me leave. I'm forty-five but you wouldn't believe the way I'm regressing, visibly regressing.

He says to himself, I haven't got any business being here. What was I looking for, anyway?

Kurt Bayer takes a red packet from his pocket, pulls a cigarette from it, lights it and swivels towards Lancelot, who sits there, turned to stone. Kurt Bayer contemplates him for a moment. Then he picks up his beer and an ashtray, and comes to sit down opposite pillar-of-salt Lancelot.

Kurt Bayer smiles and his face is transformed into a complex network of wrinkles – it reminds Lancelot of the cracks in a salt lake or a diagram of electronic components. He wonders, Do women like this sort of man? (He has fairly old-fashioned ideas on the subject, still thinking only men like Cary Grant can boast any degree of success, he thinks more effortless elegance than crumpled alcoholism.)

What a coincidence, Kurt Bayer exclaims, managing to inject into his voice how obviously this has absolutely nothing to do with chance. He offers a cigarette to Lancelot, who accepts it. (Lancelot has not smoked for two years, last time it happened he was on the veranda with Irina, she sniffed the air and asked:

What's that sort of kerosene smell, is there a plane falling out of the sky?

No, it's my lighter, Lancelot replied, waving his Zippo. He looked Irina in the eye and she emitted a little laugh to make quite sure Lancelot didn't go thinking she wasn't joking, and Lancelot felt he was sinking into a dark abyss, and thought to himself, I think I'll give up smoking.)

I work over the road, Kurt Bayer says, pointing to his red shopfront.

Lancelot keeps smiling, he has lost his voice.

It's better than breeding pointers, says Bayer, and the climate's warmer.

Lancelot nods, still mute.

What are you doing round here? Bayer asks.

And, as Lancelot gives no reply, he speaks for him:

Oh yes, of course, you lived in Camerone before you went and buried yourself in Inuit country...

Lancelot creases his eyelids to show he appreciates the witticism.

Is there something wrong? Bayer enquires, gesticulating towards his own throat. Polyps, thyroid, lost your voice...?

Lancelot coughs slightly and uses his vocal cords as if he has just had a brand new set grafted on, he speaks cautiously, listening carefully to what he is saying.

I'm happy to see you, he says.

Me too me too me too, Bayer replies, taking a sip from his beer. It's been ages...

Lancelot crosses his arms and announces:

Irina's dead.

The other man puts on a show of astonishment, widening his crinkled eyes, leaving his hand suspended in mid-air, cigarette between thumb and forefinger, No? he blurts, and that no is dragged out over several kilometres, creating a sort of noooooooooo... with a progressive extinction of intensity, distress mingled with amazement.

I'm so sorry, he adds.

And Lancelot thinks, That's right, that's right, and you don't even want to know how it happened.

That's tough, Bayer epitaphs.

He shakes his head, like an actor who has learned to portray devastation but whose sorrow, because we are now on the thirtieth take, is short on authenticity.

Did you have her buried?

Lancelot sits up with a jolt, he is surprised so many people are interested to know what happened to Irina's body.

Cremated.

I see. Bayer nods. Lancelot convinces himself the man looks relieved. Bayer goes on, I only ask because I used to be an embalmer.

Lancelot looks outside, the street is empty, he can feel himself palpitating like sugar in sunlight, he turns to Bayer and asks slowly when he practised this mortuary activity. Bayer says it was long before the escalators and pointer breeding, and he stopped at the time of the great heat wave – he ended up working round the clock.

Bayer peers at his beer and adds that at the time he often handled unusual deaths.

In fact I specialized in unusual deaths, he says.

Bayer starts to explain how he had to pick people up off aeroplanes on their way back from the islands, people who could think of nothing better to do than go scuba diving and fishing for grouper fish, only to hop straight onto the plane back home, with the grouper still twitching. But the difference in pressure produced air bubbles in their blood, tiny fatal air bubbles. Straight to the heart.

Bang. Bayer laughs.

Lancelot thinks about all the grouper fish which must have ended up rotting in the hold, no one would have thought it right to eat them and the poor things would have died for nothing.

There was this guy, Bayer goes on, who stole a jet engine from a military base in the middle of the desert. He tinkered the thing into his own car and when he set off the tyres exploded instantly. His contraption had done more than two Gs in two hundred metres (Bayer emits an engine sound and mimes the scene with his arms). He landed in the side of the mountain, twenty-five metres off the ground, he literally burrowed into the mountain, all that was left was a small hunk of carcass and some teeth. At first we thought the metal we found was from the cabin of an aeroplane that had crashed there. Then we realized it was a car.

Lancelot realizes he already knows this story, he is not

sure whether it is one of those contemporary myths people tell each other, claiming these things happened to a friend of their brother-in-law's cousin. Lancelot remembers the one about crocodiles in the New York sewers, and the man who bungee-jumped on octopus tentacles.

It's like that story, Bayer goes on, about people bungee-jumping from Manatet Bridge on octopus tentacles.

Lancelot swallows hard and thinks to himself, this bugger's leading me by the nose, he's fucking leading me by the nose.

I dealt with the guy who completely exploded in the rapids. Not a pretty sight.

Lancelot jumps to attention, it was Irina who told him all these stories, it suddenly comes back to him, he thinks to himself, Funerals (Irina's favourite expletive), it was Irina who told me about all this stuff... there were loads of others... there was the one about the man committing suicide...

And one time, Bayer continues, as if reading Lancelot's mind, a man threw himself from the top of a building...He leaves a letter explaining what the problem is, chooses the tallest building in town, climbs up on the roof and hup, he takes the jump. All round the first floor there was a net to catch stuff the inhabitants chucked out of their windows, to stop it falling on people eating out on the terrace of the restaurant at the foot of the building. That net could have saved his life. But up on the third floor, a jealous husband

(Jealous? thinks Lancelot, Irina didn't mention that detail when she told him the story) arguing with his wife picks up a shotgun, aims at his wife, who's standing in front of the window, and fires, the bullet misses his wife but gets the jumper, who was falling past at that exact moment. The guy's killed on the spot. He's already dead when he lands in the safety net. His family took the jealous husband to court for manslaughter. They won the case. Unbelievable, isn't it?

Unbelievable, Lancelot manages grimly.

All at once Bayer seems to realize how incongruous his topic of conversation is. He pauses, then drinks the last mouthful of his beer and adds:

It's hearing Irina's dead that's put me in this state. I feel a bit shaky. In a macabre mood.

For a few minutes neither of them utters a word. They stare at their glasses, then look out at the street, they both look dismayed.

And Tralala? asks Lancelot. How's she?

Bayer raises his eyebrows and says with apparent reluctance:

She's still with her aunt. She seems to like it there. She writes to me, she's learnt to use a fountain pen. Would you believe it, a fountain pen? Mind you, those lunatics practically write with quills in their sect. For now, the littl'un's found what she needs there. But I'm sure when she's twelve she won't be able to hack them any longer and she'll come back to her old dad.

Bayer leans back against his chair, he talked about Tralala almost mechanically, as if he had repeated those sentences dozens of times. Eventually he says, Come on, let's get out of here, he is now floundering in bottomless sadness, I'll give you a lift, he adds. Bayer waves his hand at the waitress. Lancelot gets up and follows Bayer out onto the street. They cross the road and head for Bayer's car, walking slowly as if each carrying a colossal lead structure on his shoulders.

TWENTY-SEVEN

Lancelot fell apart that evening in front of Kurt-Klaus Bayer.

It was like falling asleep in a vast, viscous body with white fluids sploshing about inside it. That is what Lancelot said to himself, I'm inside a monstrous great body. I'm never going to get out of all this bile and fat.

He went in up to his knees when, during the course of the evening, Kurt Bayer announced that he had been a member of the Cric in his youth.

The Cric.

A really radical anti-vivisection movement, Irina's false father had called it.

You've had quite a few jobs, Lancelot ventured cautiously, feeling as if his mouth were full of ether, what did you do before the dead and the dogs and the escalators?

I killed chickens in an abattoir in the south, then I was a nurse in a neurological unit, Bayer answered, watching his ice cubes swilling in the bottom of his glass and appearing to enjoy the clinking sound they made.

Lancelot went in up to his navel.

He heaved a great sigh. It was an inaudible sigh, something deflating inside his ribcage, something which was punctured and emptied itself and turned into cloying nothingness.

Kurt Bayer had known Irina a long time.

A whole fortified castle built of matchsticks was collapsing. Silently and definitively.

Bayer and Lancelot were hitting the bottle in a dive Bayer knew well (grim, red as a brothel and damp as a cellar). Lancelot, who never drank, could tell he was going to start sobbing. A possibility that made him apathetic; he told himself, Whatever it's going to be, let it happen. His world was threatening total ruin. Lancelot's sorrow was already making his shoulders shake with jerking spasms. Bayer was beginning to go a bit hazy. His outline was shifting and his voice came and went on a capricious tide.

How could anyone know so little about the person they live with?

That was the question Lancelot put to Bayer.

How could anyone know so little about the person they live with?

Lancelot started repeating the question to a disturbing rhythm which suggested his nerves would give out at any minute.

So Bayer put his hand on the back of Lancelot's

neck (and Lancelot interpreted the gesture both as an attempt at reassurance and as a threat), and whispered, Don't worry, Paul, whatever happens, don't worry about a thing.

TWENTY-EIGHT

Kurt Bayer does not drive Lancelot back to his boarding house near the fire station, but takes him home. Lancelot talks incoherently and his head rocks backwards and forwards as if mounted on a faulty spring. His mouth has been stuffed with some sort of substance, it seems to him, something gelatinous and sticky like a sea spider's innards, he says it several times, opening his mouth and pointing at his throat, Shea shpider, shea shpider. Bayer nods, driving with one hand and opting for a soothing tone of voice and a litany of lullabies, It's going to be OK it's going to be OK we're nearly there it's going to be OK, leaning forwards and rummaging in the footwell with his free hand to find a plastic bag in case of an incident, still trying to keep an eye on the road despite his inappropriate position and the number of stickers (several smiling suns declaiming in Esperanto: Nuclear no thanks!) round the outside of the windscreen, like the beginnings of a mosaic, and carrying on with his, It's going to be OK it's going to be OK we're nearly there, seeing double or even triple himself at times but being so accustomed to this multiplication of the world that he copes with it, aiming somewhere in the middle and coming off pretty well.

They arrive outside Bayer's house. It is a pokey place and its only attractive feature is a smooth pale plane tree, square and symmetrical with centennial proportions, overshadowing the front part of the cottage.

It is just before dawn in the outskirts of Camerone.

Bayer extracts Lancelot from the car and carries him to his bed. He says, I've got to go, I'll be back later, get some rest, and Lancelot feels a rush of giddiness like when you climb a staircase in the dark and think there is one more stair after the last one, your foot flounders for a moment, suspended above this phantom stair, and Lancelot topples, he thinks he nods and says something decipherable but nothing convincing actually comes from his mouth. He goes to sleep and Bayer leaves.

When Lancelot comes round he lies motionless with his arms spread wide in the middle of Bayer's bed, staring at the white ceiling where the damp has produced patches of mossy vegetation, he sneezes five times in succession, swears, then rolls onto his side, Hey what, what is it? he murmurs, screwing up his eyes and trying to remember. On the stool beside the bed is a glass of water and two aspirins; he thinks, Am I at Bayer's house? He tries to, but everything breaks up and scatters like beads of mercury dispersing, he just wants, but it doesn't work.

He swallows down the two aspirins and the glass of water.

He makes an effort to get up but still feels dizzy, he has pins and needles in the tips of his fingers and toes and dick, it is an unfamiliar sensation and he concentrates on it (Is it all going to go necrotic and fall off? Is that it?), he puts his feet squarely on the floor, slides over the bed to get closer to the wall, and gets up.

I'm forty-five and I've been on my first bender. He could almost cry. He always portrayed his sobriety as asceticism. In fact he was just too frightened of losing face.

You were fucking terrified, Irina would have said.

Lancelot looks outside, huddling his head between his shoulders and screwing his eyes up as tightly as possible, it must be about midday, the king of plane trees looks like a stone statue, there is not a breath of wind. Lancelot experiences his first satisfaction of the day by thinking of the cold in Catano and comparing it with the mild air in Camerone, he tells himself he'll count these small pleasures throughout the day.

There is a note from Bayer on the kitchen table: GONE TO WORK. YOU CAN STAY HERE.

Lancelot makes himself a cup of tea, he finds a saucepan and some teabags at the back of a cupboard, puts the water on to boil and sits at the pale yellow Formica table, facing the window and the plane tree, he sighs, he can hear noises from a building site outside, they are putting up a new building right next door, Lancelot feels calm and focused, the tea is not as dusty as he thought it would be, that is his second pleasure of the day.

TWENTY-NINE

Lancelot spends this first day sitting in Bayer's house listening to the radio spluttering, and getting himself back on track by mulling over the muddle things have got into.

He is not sure why, but this muddle keeps bringing him back to his and Irina's wedding. At first he does not see the connection. There should be no connection.

One day she just announced she would like to be called Irina Rubinstein. And Lancelot could find no objection to marrying the love of his life – even though his unhappy first marriage might have put him off.

She said, You married Elisabeth, and that's really not fair.

So they got married in Catano. Bayer and Tralala were there, because it was before they both moved away, along with someone from the newspaper where Lancelot worked.

Irina was just back from covering a story in the Aral Sea, the things she had seen there had outraged her at first, then plunged her into a silent stupor. She was still in this cataleptic state when they celebrated their wedding.

She talked very little but smiled a great deal, she seemed slightly absent and not emotionally involved at all.

Lancelot thought to himself, What a funny woman I'm marrying.

And, as he always did, he felt a stab of pride watching her move about the room (her perfect Redder Than Red lipstick, her white coat and fur hat, little old-fashioned details which gave Lancelot the illusion he was wedded to a diva), he watched her and told himself, It's me, Lancelot, who's marrying this woman, and he could not believe it, he would have liked his mother to see him from wherever she was (in limbo?) and congratulate him on his choice (choice?), he knew she would have loved discussing the desperate state of the planet with Irina but would have warned him against marrying such an alluring creature, She'll drive you to distraction, she would have said. And would inevitably have added, A jealous man like you doesn't choose a woman like her, it's a big mistake and it's bound to make you unhappy, and the subtext of these words was that she felt he was at a disadvantage, she would have suggested a variety of more accessible consolations and would have comforted him in her usual melancholic way.

Lancelot felt he was braving something by marrying Irina.

Lancelot had not chosen anything.

When they got home after eating in a restaurant with Bayer, Tralala and the man from the newspaper – a

macrobiotic restaurant, which it had to be, they had to go all
the way to Milena to find the place, it served seeds and
nothing derived from animal sources, Nothing with eyes
and teeth, Lancelot joked, and Irina stroked his forearm and
told him it was much worse than he would have thought
because the milk they used in their pastries was almond
milk, and there was no question of using eggs in any of their
dishes – when they got home, then, he carried Irina over the
threshold in his arms, and laid her on the sofa, she tossed off
her hat, coat, stockings, shoes and dress, and pronounced
the order, Fuck me (so those were her first words as a married woman inside their house), she got up and leant on the
table to look at her profile in the big mirror hanging on the
wall, presenting her buttocks to Lancelot. He saw the reflec-
tion of her breasts and her dark nipples hanging down to the
table, and the sight of them aroused him violently, he did
not get undressed but took Irina from behind and they
watched themselves doing it, he liked seeing his hands on
Irina's arse and his dick penetrating her and also his face in
the mirror, and Irina cried but that was nothing unusual,
and she laughed and they said they loved each other and she
announced, I'm getting out the champagne, and they
clinked glasses, she sat on the sofa still naked, Lancelot
drank one glass and Irina put away the rest, and he sensed
how sad and content she was, he was suddenly aware of the
contradictions she struggled with, and thought, Now I'm
helpless but overjoyed too.

Then he thought, Didn't I see her, while I was taking her, picking at the dead skin on her thumb with her index finger? Is that really something you can do when you're making love? Do I bore her and is she just indulging me when she joins in?

Lancelot is alone at Bayer's house. He racks his brains, going round in circles and no longer sure what to think about sex with Irina (after making love with him she would ask, Was it good, the sex? It was as if she had not quite mastered the language, she sounded like an embarrassed little Russian whore).

A diffuse sort of fear clutches him when he goes back over that wedding-night fuck. He tries to picture the living room when he left Catano. Was the big mirror still up on the wall? Hadn't it vanished? He gives a feeble groan. How could he fail, if this went on, to feel offended by a world (or his own senses) that was (or were) so unreliable?

THIRTY

Bayer very soon reveals two important things to Lancelot. How to make TNT and the fact that he and Irina remained close friends for many years without revealing anything of their past relationship to Lancelot.

What sort of close friends? asks Lancelot.

Bayer shrugs.

We weren't sleeping together if that's what you want to know.

That's what I wanted to know.

She loved you very much, she wouldn't have left you for anything in the world, she talked about you the whole time, she used to say, We're made for each other. Do you see what that means? She used to say, He goes and gets me strawberries when I want strawberries, he takes me in his arms when I need comforting, he listens to me and talks to me, we're made for each other.

Lancelot's mother would have said, You can shove that in your pocket and fold your hankie over it.

Lancelot wonders, Can I cope with listening to everything this man has to tell me?

After that comes a flood of revelations.

Lancelot holds tight and hangs on. The first few times he closes his eyes to picture his treasure, he would do anything in the world not to forget her face, he reconstructs it starting with the left eye (very black irises under neat eyelashes, dark skin with brown marks at the temples – at times she said they were because of the sun and at others a result of nutritional deficiencies in her youth when she wanted to weigh less than a fistful of cotton – thin lips and a slightly overshot lower jaw, which gave her face a carnivorous and imperceptibly aggressive quality, long dark hair coiled up in a (tumbling) bun, a small chin and symmetrical bone structure almost showing beneath the skin, Don't forget, she used to say, beauty is all to do with bone structure). Lancelot is afraid the memory of his sweetheart his love his precious will alter as he listens to what Bayer has to say, he is prepared to modify what he knows about her but not to lose her at any cost.

He says to himself, After all, what's so appalling about what I've heard?

Is it that bad to discover that my beloved wife was still seeing a former lover she used to – and apparently still did – lead a wild life with?

Come on come on.

Can I carry on living now that I know that?

Can I carry on living now that I know she wanted to exclude me from all this, to lie to me and fabricate complex structures of alibis and dissimulations, to leave me utterly mystified, to dupe me so she could carry on seeing Bayer, talking to him on the phone and employing the same ruses as an adulterous wife? Is it more acceptable being the sanctimonious hypocrite in this farce given that actual bedding there was none?

What sort of business were you both in? Lancelot asks, sounding like someone who feels both legitimate and ridiculed.

Nothing reprehensible, my liege, Bayer replies in the appropriate tone of voice. Or at least not in the way you would mean it. It was to do with political ideals.

This comment reduces Lancelot to silence, making him feel more helpless than ever. Is it possible to know nothing about or to minimize to this extent the political commitments of the person you live with? Surely I myself am guilty of being so blind or so latently but insistently contemptuous that I couldn't see my lovely one clearly? Wasn't she in constant despair at my condescending attitude to the whole question of her political commitments? Didn't she resign herself to keeping the truth about her activities from me because I responded with patronizing amusement every time she took up the cause of some new global catastrophe?

Should I still smash Bayer's face in (right now, just like that, for the good of my soul), should I cave in his remaining teeth (including the golden ones), should I bury him alive and leave just his head sticking out of the sand, and launch my galloping horse (my horse?) at him to knock it off, should I drive a blade as long as my arm into his heart?

Lancelot thinks to himself, I'd really like to punch him.

Yes, that's it, make a gash in his brow and watch over several days as his nose goes blue, then tends towards browny yellow, roasting, caramelizing, turning into burnt butter.

I'd love to punch him.

He looks at Bayer and keeps saying to himself, I'd love to punch him.

THIRTY-ONE

A shadow lives on the faces of those who have lost someone.
The shadow of a climbing plant. It grows in spite of them,
when they think no one is watching; it bathes their features
in absence, gravity and bafflement. A discreet demon living
on their faces. Hiding the moment anyone looks at it.

THIRTY-TWO

When Bayer opens the door to his house on the third evening he finds Lancelot inert as a plaster cast, sitting waiting for him at the table, hands crossed over the pale yellow Formica with a glass of cold water positioned slightly too far from his hands. Bayer says hello and Lancelot asks, by way of a preamble (and as he asks the question he thinks to himself, I shouldn't have launched in with this, he screws up his face with embarrassment, feeling ridiculous, but does not know how else to tackle the subject, he is so powerless, bogged down in silt with great clodhoppers on his feet, a clumsy lump, awkward and hunchbacked and desperate to have an answer to what he is asking):

Is Tralala Irina's daughter?

Once over the initial surprise, Bayer starts to laugh, he laughs so hard that Lancelot shrinks back like a winkle. Bayer laughs and eventually manages something along the lines of, We're not in a soap opera, and Lancelot does not laugh because he is not sure what Bayer means and cannot see why this suggestion is any more incongruous than everything he has already been told about Irina since her death (can it be called 'death'?).

No, no, no, Tralala's mother really is the beautiful red-headed creature Lancelot saw in a photograph on the chest of drawers in Bayer's house.

Irina couldn't have children, explains Bayer, it never lasted.

What never lasted? Lancelot asks, tensing his jaw.

Babies.

In what way didn't they last?

Inside her. (Bayer opens the fridge and takes a beer, he comes and sits opposite Lancelot, rolling the can across his forehead to cool it, he does not seem to think Lancelot is being particularly stupid but it is hard to know what is really going on behind that funny, creased face. Still, as if not convinced Lancelot has understood, he adds:) In her womb. She had one miscarriage after another. It would last a month or two then she'd lose the baby.

Did she want to have a child with you?

We were very young, we didn't really know what we were doing, we would split up, then get back together again (Bayer takes a swig of his beer, wipes his lips and pulls a face). I'm not sure you want to hear all this.

Bayer gets up. He says, I need to have a look at the well. Check the fuckers opposite haven't cracked the shaft with all their underground car parks.

Lancelot follows him outside. He helps Bayer lift the slab of concrete off the well and lay it down in the courtyard.

Do you know someone called Romero? Lancelot asks, standing on the concrete while Bayer probes the depths of the well with his torch.

I've got to go down, Bayer grumbles.

Can you answer my question?

Bayer sits down on the edge of the well and looks at Lancelot.

Is Romero the one with pharmaceuticals labs in every country?

Yes.

Why do you ask?

Just because.

They fall silent.

Lancelot would like to tell Bayer something he does not know about Irina, the idea titillates him, so he makes a stab at it:

You know Irina went and looked at a lot of houses. I wanted to see one of them but it had gone up in smoke. It belonged to Romero.

The guy from the labs.

The guy from the labs.

Lancelot feels crestfallen. It is impossible to tell whether Bayer already knows about this or even participated in pulverizing the house in question.

Lancelot sits down next to Bayer on the coping, with his

back to the well. A dark smell of slugs and old paper comes up from the well. Lancelot tilts back his head to look at the sky. He wipes his hands on his trousers and starts to explain how a man claiming to be Irina's father came to see him in Catano after her death (still very cautious about pronouncing this word, as if tentatively using a freshly scarred limb).

Her father died of cirrhosis ages ago, Bayer says shaking his head.

Ah-ha, I thought as much.

And what did he look like, this man who came to see you?

A retired general.

Is that all?

He stood very upright. Maybe sixty years old. Or a bit more. He knew her well...

How do you mean?

I don't know... He gave me details about her childhood, he told me about the Cric and about you, he said he and Irina had fallen out.

Of course.

Of course, Lancelot concludes.

The two men sit in silence, they look at his majesty the plane tree, Bayer points to it, It's the oldest one in town. They fall silent again, Bayer hitches his combat trousers up to the knee, his hair is a little dirtier than the day before, giving it a peculiar silvery sheen like strips of old leather, he looks as relaxed as a Siamese cat sitting there on the coping stones. He really does not seem to want to go down into the well and check for cracks.

Lancelot says:

She knew how to make bombs.

Loads of people know how to make bombs, Bayer replies.

Lancelot notices that you could count to a hundred in the pauses between them speaking.

Not me, he says.

There is another pause of a hundred seconds.

I could teach you, if you like, Bayer offers, screwing up his eyes as if the light flickering through the branches were bothering him.

Lancelot takes his time before replying:

I don't know.

He stays there contemplating Bayer's tree, thinking, I'm going to like it here. He immerses himself in minutely observing the paler patches on the plane tree's trunk, they look like psoriasis on an old woman's hands, but Lancelot sees them as clouds, letting his rather clichéd imagination bring them to life, succumbing to sentimentality (a fairly pronounced tendency of his) by enjoying the tweeting of a common house sparrow, quite prepared to take it for a nightingale (and he can only hear the thing intermittently between the sound of pneumatic drills from the nearby building site).

I don't know, he says again. He feels good, never wants to move from here, would like to stay sitting as close as possible to Bayer because talking to Bayer is like being a schoolboy again and talking to friends who share a secret inclination, and mentioning that special girl without revealing what particular status she has in your heart, and your head spins the minute anyone speaks the name of this hidden love.

It's a great place here, he eventually says out loud.

THIRTY-THREE

Lancelot has come with Bayer to the shopping centre which takes up the first two storeys of the Sun Tower – an office building with mirror-effect sealed windows, there is no way of opening them, you'll have to make do with air conditioning, going down with bronchitis and making a hole in the ozone layer.

The escalator leading up from the car parks has broken down.

Bayer has swapped his name for Klaus Meyer. He could have chosen something exotic like Pedro de Lucia but such a radical change would definitely have felt like a doubly mean trick. Change your name, by all means, but keep a surname similar to the old one to avoid feeling completely different at the sound of this new name and this deception practised several times a day. He has come with all his repairman's paraphernalia, accompanied by Lancelot, his toolbox-carrying assistant.

He said, I need someone with me, watch closely how

I do it and you'll learn very quickly.

Lancelot realizes that for a long time he thought Irina was joking when she said Bayer had abandoned his pointers to take care of escalators. At the time he had not really succeeded in believing anything of the sort.

And now here is Lancelot crouching on the heavy-duty parquet floor of a shopping centre (boards twelve centimetres thick stuck closely side by side, they should last about a hundred and twenty years, we'll all be dead or as good as between now and then, every one of us schlepping about on this floor will have turned to dust and ant shit, but this fucking flooring will still be here shifting subtly on its backing strips and sneering at our perishable organs), next to Bayer in his black combats and red T-shirt with blue flock letters saying Tralala Fixitall (with stars dotting the i's), Lancelot concentrating on his new profession, far away from Doctor Epstein's pills and Detective Schneider's insinuations, the detective who dared (she dared!) to suspect him of eliminating his princess, far away from the interminable freezing cold nights and the indigenous vegetation (nothing but fir trees fir trees fir trees) of those northern lands, Lancelot himself not sure what has fuelled his peculiar satisfaction in finding Bayer again, in knowing that this man once slept with his beloved even though he has always been the most jealous man on earth (but the most credulous too), and in sharing his huge sorrow with this alcoholic pyrotechnician.

When it is time for a coffee break Lancelot sits on one of the blue plastic benches supplied for the public, chewing on the sandwich he brought with him (cucumber, wholemeal bread) and looking at the pot plants that eke out an existence in this place where their only nourishment seems to be small beads of fired earth, he drinks his can of orange juice (bitter taste and crab-flavoured froth), then listens religiously to the messages on his mobile, with one finger in his ear so as not to be disturbed by the shopping centre's mawkish music. There is a message from Detective Schneider asking him to get in touch with her as soon as he can, she says he is impossible to get hold of, the police must be able to contact him, there is nothing new in the enquiry but she needs to talk to him, she even says she sent someone to his house and they saw that he had cleared the floor, which he finds suspect (she sounds annoyed and threatening); there is a message from Doctor Epstein reminding Lancelot he needs to go back to see him for his treatment (he sounds annoyed and accusatory). And a mass of messages from Marie Marie. Listening to them one after another has a surprising effect. Her voice changes, she sounds anxious in some, then goes back to being playful in others, she asks whether he still wants to sell his house because she might well have found a buyer, she complains after a meeting with an aggressive client, she comments on the snow and the starry sky, refers to her boss, her son, the father of her son and her boyfriend (who are, apparently, two different people but this distinction is not as clear as it seems to be), she mentions her mother (who lives a long way away from her and calls her at night because of the time difference but cannot say anything on the phone), she sometimes talks about death, about the pain she feels here in her chest, then goes on to something else, she calls him from her car and from restaurants where she has lunch, he can hear the thrum of voices or the engine. The closer the messages get to the present, the more personal and, paradoxically, the more anonymous they become, she is no longer talking to Lancelot, merely depositing her sadness for the day in a little box and closing the lid gently so as not to wake it.

Lancelot switches off his mobile without deleting Marie Marie's messages. Then he goes back over to Bayer, who is still tinkering away next to the gaping escalator.

Are you going to mend it? Lancelot whispers as if there were enemy microphones hidden in the depressive plants.

Bayer shrugs his shoulders and looks at it, frowning, perhaps trying to shed some light on Lancelot's intentions.

What do you think? he replies. I've got to earn my living.

Then he smiles, as if amused by Lancelot's budding infatuation with clandestine activities.

And, perhaps disappointed or – more likely – reassured, Lancelot thinks to himself, This is my new job. My New Job. And his heart feels quite light in his chest. He starts enjoying Bayer's company and his regular allusions to his dick (It's long and hard today, or Stretch that pink strap out tight then let it go off on its own), even savouring the shopping-centre version of *Hotel California* playing on a loop through the loud speakers, appreciating the soft-soled presence of some security guards who come to chat and joke with Bayer and wander off again, wearing their armbands saying Security with obvious pleasure, Lancelot feels he is in his place, almost wants to know nothing more about Irina, feeling it less and less vital to inform Bayer that someone poisoned her before throwing her off the bridge, not wanting to make or endure any more revelations for now, satisfied with calmly digesting what he has learned so far.

THIRTY-FOUR

At first living with Irina was like a form of torment.

It was not that easy having chosen a woman who had all the qualities of a circus rider. Lancelot was sometimes overwhelmed by Irina's beauty.

That certainly was true when they still lived in Camerone. Because she knew a lot of people and it was hard to ignore the fact that Irina had lived in the city with other men, had slept with them, been involved in shady dealings with some, enjoyed near-intimate relationships (just a few confidences and conspiratorial giggles over a cappuccino) with others, because there was always the possibility of her running into one of them in the street and, nostalgia being what it is, they might have spent a while digging up the past with little smiles hovering over their features, and when she came home Lancelot would have noticed this change, like a light turned in a different direction, she would have spoken with detachment (because she knew you had to sound detached to say things like this to Lancelot; she would not have had the heart to hide her fortuitous meeting from him but would have wanted to avoid any combustion calcination oxidation on his part), so, as she took off her sandals or washed her hands, she would have called from the kitchen so that her voice carried to the living room (and so that Lancelot could not see her face and detect the effort she was making precisely in order to adopt this detached tone), she would have said, I bumped into Charles, or (because people had weird ridiculous names in Irina's past) I bumped into Minimax or Tororo, and Lancelot would have felt his heart fill with acid, he would have resented her (for not avoiding Tororo or Minimax or perhaps for having a life before him), and the evening would have been irretrievably ruined.

There was also no neglecting the fact that the clement climate in Camerone encouraged women (and forced Irina) to wear virtually transparent clothes (to walk about almost naked). Lancelot tried to get her to see sense in the morning by warning her about the sneaky nip in the air which would catch her out during the course of the day if she didn't put on a scarf or, better still, swap her peculiarly plunging crossover top for a navy blue polo neck. Usually Irina made no reply to Lancelot's comments, she carried on getting ready to go out as if he had addressed her on a frequency she could not hear, she kissed him and went off to her meetings, and Lancelot stayed in the living room, eyes wide, feeling aggrieved and dismayed.

Irina often looked for editing jobs while she was waiting

for funding for documentaries she had suggested. Lancelot found it difficult not to fantasize about what an editing suite might look like, and about the budding complicity between Irina and her alter egos in such a confined and ill-lit space.

That would have been grounds enough for torture.

But the worst thing was when Irina took him to parties with her. The prospect of spending his time with acquaintances of Irina's, isolated in the kitchen of a tiny apartment, or at best a balcony heaving with lush plants, drinking raspberry-flavoured punch while he waited for her to stop dancing did not do a great deal for him. But the thought of letting her go on her own suited him no better.

They always arrived at strangers' houses slightly late because he showed such reluctance to put on a presentable shirt, it could take him hours; he hoped, by procrastinating like this, to convince Irina that leaving the house and going somewhere as noisy and crowded as that could not in any way be considered a pleasant evening. She waited patiently for him on the doorstep as if she did not understand what this was all about, she wore heels so perfect and so pointed he would groan with desire, and a dress so low-cut he could weep with despair, she fiddled with her keys while she waited, and their jingling cut right through Lancelot's stomach, he felt trapped, both devastated and utterly under his beauty's spell.

Often they did not exchange a single word on the way there. She took his hand but he said nothing. They got on the tram, and the noise and crowds meant they avoided any confrontation. When they rang on Irina's friends' doorbell (and you could already hear the muffled bass of a stolid sound system), she smiled at him (a feeble smile, granted, but one that said, or so Lancelot hoped, I care about you, I don't resent you for this, and Lancelot wanted to repent for creating the dissent between them but it was too late), then their host opened the door, recognized Irina and squealed like a weasel, Irina herself would start giggling and would suddenly speak Spanish or Mandarin, or God knows what else, Lancelot watched her metamorphose, he felt he was being expelled at the speed of light to the furthest depths of the galaxy, she jumped on the spot with excitement and they stepped into the overpopulated place (which was not an apartment but two or three rooms in a housing project whose walls had been knocked through with a sledge-hammer).

Lancelot then found himself surrounded by a gang of lefties, militants, ecologists and refugees, all drinking and dancing wherever they happened to be, sometimes there was even one singing, and Lancelot wanted to disappear, yes, one of them was singing, it was terrifying, and people went into ecstasies or did not listen at all, and Lancelot thought, The world's going to the dogs. Lancelot landed up in the communal kitchen on the landing, his buttocks in a draught as he perched on the sink, chatting to a dwarf editorial writer whose name vaguely meant something to him, and he saw Irina flitting across his field of vision and could no longer concentrate on what the journalist was saying to him, he could hear Irina talking to her friends, she had a drink in her hand, she gave him a little wave and he could see from the look in her eye that she was completely out of it, he would have liked to follow her but could not, he had to make her believe he had formed a friendship with the dwarf journalist, he glimpsed her dancing in the corridor then coming back over towards him, she kissed him in passing and carried on nattering with her girlfriends, he sometimes caught a snatch of conversation and felt he was teetering on the edge of a precipice, it was like leafing through a women's magazine where one page buttonholes you with: Should we worry about melting glaciers? and the next double-page spread tempts you with the best far-flung marine spas on earth.

He told himself, They're modern women.

And while the dwarf journalist carried on talking at great speed, as if afraid of being interrupted, Lancelot kept telling himself, They're modern women, and the guy had given up breathing between sentences, for fear of being cut off midstream, and Lancelot, who was not listening and knew how not to listen with a degree of panache by appearing to do so, kept on thinking, They're modern women, as if he had pinpointed some fundamental truth.

He never experienced this helpless feeling of abandonment before meeting Irina. But he guessed it had precious little to do with her. It was just a creature that lived there, lurking in his inner jungle, and had been waiting for the appropriate combination of circumstances to come out of the undergrowth.

When they moved to Catano things calmed down, Lancelot's jealousy changed into a simple need to locate Irina precisely. When she travelled abroad, he did not feel particularly abandoned, he just waited for her, he now knew she would come back, she was punctual and considerate, and called regularly. He was only afraid she would meet another man, all he worried about was episodic fucks, sort of makeshift fucks, vaguely constitutional goings-on included in his concept of journeys. If he started thinking about this his mind went round in circles and churned over thousands of inter-cut images of mucous membranes and seeping members, so he had learnt to keep them at a distance, like a trap he must not fall into. In the days immediately after Irina had set off he would count out his every step as he walked towards some distant destination, ever cautious and on the alert for his mind's peculiar impulses, he went out very early in the morning to tramp through the cold, going under the Omoko bridge and watching the sun come up, he cut through the Catano forest and came back cleansed of his suspicions. Sometimes, in these early days, when he was still very fragile, he came across a box of matches on the shelves over the sink, a box of matches from a bar in some faraway town, and he wondered how it had ended up there, whether Irina had put it there (in which case what man had she been to the bar with, because she obviously could not have gone there alone and her acolyte of the time had to be a man) or if it was a rep selling white goods, aluminium windows or hypo-allergenic carpeting who had come to their house in Lancelot's absence, when he had gone out on an errand, and who, as well as smoking in their living room and forgetting his box of matches, pleasured Irina on the conjugal bed (or next to it).

Lancelot realized he had a problem with things. He let them get inside his head and circulate freely through his feelings, he had trouble erecting barriers between who he was and the hostility of things.

So he took one or two harmless medicines and calmed down, and after that he was back to being a more serene sort of man – the one who watched opossums in the camphor tree in Camerone.

THIRTY-FIVE

Lancelot is sleeping in Bayer's bed.

Bayer is sleeping on the sofa.

He says the living room is always wreathed in a thick fug from his Cravens and it wouldn't be right to make Lancelot spend the night there.

The living room has a door to the outside and if you are in the bedroom you have to come through it to get out. The bedroom has only a tiny window with bars which makes it feel like a monk's cell, the floor is concrete, covered with coconut matting so rough that walking barefoot over it could be mistaken for a Zen observance.

It's a good spot, Bayer told him.

And Lancelot wondered, A good spot for what?

At night you can hear the hiss of the motorway, goods trains squealing along the railway track and, before sunrise, the rowdy wake-up calls of the feathered population in the plane tree, a cacophony of cries and squabbles and rustling foliage and score-settling and odes to dawn, like something from a music-hall show in its heyday.

Lancelot wakes at five o'clock. A time for wild animals. It is inscribed right there, in his chest and the darkest, most archaic convolutions of his brain. Lancelot wakes abruptly. Checks the time by feeling about on the floor and illuminating the digital figures on the watch lying there, is thrilled by his own punctuality and lies perfectly motionless, he gets used to the dark, checks the progress of cracks on the ceiling, makes out witches' profiles in them, concentrates on the feel of the sheets under his flattened palms, listens to Bayer's noisy breathing coming through the door, and counts the seconds between his breaths, he savours the luxury of having no ties, of no longer having anyone close to him who could make him unhappy, he just likes knowing there is someone under the same roof, it adds a distinctive flavour to his loneliness. Lancelot values or tries to value the peculiar peace he has found here.

Everything seems complicated and dazzling, as if he has discovered a cave inside a glacier or been trapped in the innards of a Swiss clock.

It glitters but he does not understand any of it.

Today, at bang on five o'clock, Lancelot wakes, experiences that sweetly vertiginous moment of not knowing where he is, feels his mind and memory taking shape again, and listens to the night pulsing around him.

Someone is whispering in the next room.

He strains his ears.

He gets up as quietly as possible and hears the fridge click and purr. He walks barefoot over the abrasive matting, holds his breath, stops in the middle of the room, like a child caught out in Grandmother's footsteps, convinced someone has heard him and is going to burst into the room and tell him to mind his own business, that he's very lucky he's being put up at all while he's at a loose end, poor Lancelot, and his life's falling apart. The whispering starts again, then the sound of a lighter, an inhalation, the crumpled sigh of a cigarette being consumed (paper burning), and quieter murmurings answering the other voice, a sound you might think you cannot hear, the infrasonic vibration elephants make in the echo chamber between their eyes, something so deep it is not your ears that hear it but your ribcage that vibrates.

Lancelot peers through the doorway.

He sees Bayer sitting on his metal chair, balancing on the back legs, rocking calmly and smoking, with his ankles resting on the sill beneath an open window. There is a man sitting beside him but he is leaning towards the floor with his arms slumped on his thighs, suggesting despair or exhaustion.

His silhouetted figure is stiff and thin as a rake.

Lancelot actually feels his heart jump slightly in his chest as he recognizes this silhouette.

It is Paco Picasso.

Or whatever his real name is.

He tries to hear what they are saying, their exchanges are punctuated by long silences during which they both lose themselves in contemplating the part of the plane tree next to a street light. Lancelot catches Irina's name and asks himself, Is this man really Irina's father? Then corrects himself, No, of course not. He can feel his brain whirring like a calculator. He hears them both laugh, very discreetly and very briefly, he thinks, They're laughing at me, they fall silent again and Lancelot feels trapped, having to stay frozen like a pillar of salt. Paco is one of Irina's former lovers, he tells himself. This thought feels like a light being switched on in the dark. Those two seem to have known each other a long time. Lancelot watches them closely. He thinks, Maybe my Irina once left one for the other. And, in the light of this new information, he finds their pacifism exemplary. He is jealous of their complicity and of something else somehow connected with virility, something obscure which excludes him from the game.

He says to himself, My Irina, my lovely, my sweet, my fish, my almond, my gazelle.

Then he thinks, They're old comrades in arms, old fighters from the Cric.

He tries to remember, was Paco Picasso the man he saw in Irina's apartment the day he was hit on the head by a high-heeled shoe? This effort of memory exhausts him, he wants to go and sit down on the edge of the bed to think in relative comfort, to have a rest and go back to sleep, but he cannot bring himself to take his eyes off them. He wonders, Did she sleep with these beanpoles? These men with faces like murderers? He thinks, My Irina. He shakes his head with infinite indulgence, as if she were there before him and he were forgiving her a childish mishap – as if she had got a grass stain on her pretty new dress.

When he came to see him in Catano, this man just wanted to know what Irina's husband looked like.

That's all.

Anyway, I couldn't give a stuff.

Lancelot beats a retreat across the bedroom. He feels drained. He sees Irina's secrets as a leafy, inhabited forest – the trees are actually the long legs of funny-looking wading birds.

I couldn't give a stuff.

Lancelot sits on the edge of the bed and lets himself fall back onto the mattress.

I couldn't give a stuff.

The men stop talking out there, by the window, all of a sudden there is no sound at all outside. Lancelot hears the magical silence of the night.

It is as if everything is in such an intensely deep sleep that he might succeed in sending it to sleep.

THIRTY-SIX

An hour or so later Lancelot wakes and wonders where he is, whether he has been dreaming and what day of the week it is. It is barely light and there are already sounds coming from the next room. Lancelot goes over to the door of his bedroom. Heavy objects are being dragged across the room. It makes a dusty, rasping sound, old slippers on a concrete garage floor.

He takes a peek through the keyhole, and remembers himself as a six-year-old spying on his mother in the bathroom, excited and disgusted and terrified.

He's killed Bayer and is nicking his treasure, Lancelot tells himself.

Paco makes several trips. Then takes his cigarette, which has been burning down in the ashtray on the table.

Fuck, I've got to call the police.

Paco goes and parks himself by the window and finishes his cigarette as he looks out at the regal plane tree. He stands absolutely still.

The police are my friends.

Then he seems to pick up the thread of his thoughts, and puts out his cigarette under the tap in the sink.

The police are there to help me.

Someone calls him from outside. Not too loudly. Because it is very early and Lancelot is supposed to be asleep. Paco breathes, I'm coming, I'm coming, and Bayer has not been assassinated, he is trying to cram all the boxes Paco has hauled out of the house into the back of his van.

Where on earth have all these boxes come from? Lancelot sees the ladder lying along the kitchen wall. He manages to look upwards and catches sight of a trap door open to the attic. He had not noticed the trap door till now. Because it was hidden amongst the sections of the false ceiling and because Lancelot is not the sort of man to go looking for secret doors to clandestine attics.

Lancelot stays there, bent double with his hands on his knees, spying on them through the keyhole. They have both climbed into the van. Lancelot says to himself, I'm going to follow them. He feels excited and disgusted and terrified. He puts on some trousers and leaps into the next room the moment the van sets off. He grabs Bayer's bicycle from against the wall as if it were made of carbon fibre, amazing himself with his new-found energy, he is quick, fluent and completely awake. He hops on the bike and pedals off behind them.

The air is cool and it is still dark enough for his task of

following the van's lights to be child's play. Lancelot can feel his cheeks becoming cold and smooth, his lungs struggling then settling to the rhythm of his efforts. It is such a long time since he has taken any sort of physical exercise. He starts smiling on his bicycle, feeling deliciously jubilant, but stops smiling because the wind hurts his teeth and dries out his gums.

He cuts across Camerone and the town takes on a misty grey hue, only assuming its true light when the streetlamps go out as if someone were tearing the gauzy sheet of organza separating them from the world around them.

After half an hour the van goes into the car park of an animal-feed wholesaler. Lancelot stops the far side of the fence, not getting off the bike but clinging to the wire mesh to keep his balance. He feels alive and titillated. He sees them park, get out of the van, open the back, take out the boxes and put several of them into Paco's car – which Lancelot recognizes in a flash with his new detective's eye. Then they seem to be waiting for something, they joke, look up at the sky, The pair of them really look like a couple of crooks, they light cigarettes, They can't be transporting explosives or they'd be more careful, a car comes into the car park, Why are women always drawn to their sort? It parks close to them, Aren't they supposed to be drawn to reliable men prepared to perpetuate the race? A man gets out, they greet him and there is a repeat performance of boxes going from one vehicle to another, I actually think the most virile men (or those thought to be) aren't the best candidates for procreation. The new arrival leaves as soon as the operation is completed, Unless our animal bodies instruct males like that, the ones who attract the females, to abandon their conquests the minute the deed is done. Paco and Kurt shake hands and pat each other on the shoulder.

Lancelot feels befuddled.

Paco drives off in his car, then it is Kurt Bayer's turn to leave.

Lancelot no longer has the energy to follow by bike. He even wonders how it was possible on the way there. He heaves himself back onto the saddle and makes the return journey lost in thought. The traffic is beginning to get heavier and Lancelot pedals all the way back to Kurt Bayer's house with his head down and his knees feeling rusty.

When he arrives Kurt Bayer is drinking a cup of coffee in the kitchen with his feet up on the stool. Lancelot comes in and rests the bicycle against the wall, exactly where he found it. Kurt Bayer watches him, frowning slightly.

Have you been out? he says.

I've been out, Lancelot replies.

He hesitates between several expressions, pleasant or nasty, and stays there a moment, feeling a tad awkward and shifting from one foot to the other, his arms hanging limply and his buttocks slightly bruised by the exercise he subjected himself to so early in the morning. He gives a very feeble sigh and sits down next to Bayer.

I don't understand why Irina never talked to me about what she was up to with you, Lancelot manages, shaking his head. What was she so afraid of?

THIRTY-SEVEN

In Bayer's house there is a photo of Irina. It serves as a book-mark in a book about the Bolshevik revolution, pinioned between pages 122 and 123. In the picture Irina is about eighteen, with a dark beret on her head, her eyes almost black, with suitably heavy rings under them. She is laughing into the lens, showing off her carnivorous teeth and staring at the photographer as she brandishes a bucket of glue in one hand and a large brush in the other. She is posing in front of a brick wall on which she has clearly just stuck a poster. The glue is still damp, making it impossible to read anything on the poster. It just shines, reflecting the flash like so many mirrors. All you can see is a triumphant Irina in the middle of those great blinding flashes.

THIRTY-EIGHT

It is a Sunday, two days later, they are having breakfast together, both facing the plane tree, in fact they spend most of their time facing that plane tree, Lancelot is tipping his chair and sighing in front of his cup of tea, and Bayer is busy crumbling biscuits between his fingers as he reads the newspaper, drinks his coffee, drags on his fag and twists his ear.

Lancelot notices that the coffee table next to the sofa is no longer there. He scans the room for it and groans inwardly, Is it starting again? He tries to concentrate on something other than the heartbreaking unreliability of everyday objects.

It's nice when it's quiet, Lancelot begins.

Bayer does not reply.

The building site, I mean, he explains.

It's Sunday, of course it is, says Bayer.

They'll be at it again tomorrow…

Or not.

Or not?

Who knows? (Bayer folds his newspaper, draws the stool closer with his feet, making a sound like grit being scraped over concrete, and rests his ankles on it.)

There must be animals on that building site, says Lancelot, there always are, it disrupts them so they ferret about at night and other animals, predators, turn up to enjoy the feast...

Did Irina tell you that?

No (Lancelot shrinks back slightly, withdrawing into his shell).

They sit in silence for a moment. Lancelot has not asked a single question about Paco Picasso. The fact that he respects this need for discretion and secrecy seems to give him the reciprocal right not to mention the things he would rather not mention. He does not want to reveal anything about the poison that ate away at Irina before she took the great leap, he believes that, so long as he keeps this information to himself, the balance of strength will not be definitively against him. (While he thinks about this he says to himself, There wasn't an airbag in that fucking crate of Bayer's, there wasn't anything to lessen the impact of my lovely's face against the windscreen, he thinks, Arsehole, you couldn't buy a car with an airbag, could you?) Just then, as if he has been following the ins and outs of Lancelot's thought process, Bayer asks:

Did they find anything in the boot of my car?

Lancelot loses himself in the noise produced by half the plane tree's leaves rubbing themselves against the other half of the plane tree's leaves. All of a sudden he feels the Sunday morning air is charged with electricity, a soft rush of adrenaline constricts his heart, he closes his eyes, it is like an argument brewing. He thinks, This guy's getting on my nerves. So he says:

You're getting on my nerves.

The fuzz didn't mention anything?

You're getting on my nerves.

When I gave Irina the car at the airport there was stuff in the boot.

You piss me off.

Because theoretically, Bayer goes on, there should have been crates of music boxes.

Crates of music boxes?

The things you hang above babies' beds to send them to sleep with Schubert.

Well I never.

There should have been mikes and pink radio-cassette players for little girls, there should have been children's books with covers made of sponge and sequins. Doesn't this mean anything to you, Lancelot?

Either way, you piss me off.

Because if the fuzz had listened to the music boxes, they'd have heard that we replaced the Schubert with *Bella Ciao*, and they'd have noticed we swapped the lobotomized nonsense on the tapes for revolutionary songs.

Bayer waits a moment for the information to assume its full weight in Lancelot's mind. The latter wonders, What the hell does he want from me? Why's he started talking to me now?

They might even have opened the books, Bayer continues, and realized that the stories in them weren't to do with Goldilocks but texts with beautiful, very colourful illustrations all about children taking up arms at school to kill their teachers, stories of bear cubs being slaughtered in full view of their mothers, the one about the baby cormorant bogged down in a tide of black…

Bunch of lunatics.

But we really can't be sure of that, Bayer corrects himself. The fuzz don't open books and don't listen to music boxes.

I think they must have done.

I don't think so.

Vain bunch of crackpots.

Relatively inoffensive and not very aggressive crackpots, Bayer chuckles. Mind you, it was easier putting those books in libraries and bookshops…

Bunch of lunatics.

And putting those harmlessly subversive toys on shop shelves…

Bunch of lunatics.

It was easier and more fun than stopping tankers sinking in the Atlantic and spilling their poison. Wouldn't you say,

Lancelot? (And with that, Lancelot again wonders, Why are you telling me all this today, arsehole? Why are you spilling the beans?) It was more effective than setting off in little boats and jumping up and down in front of Japanese ships to try to save whales.

Not so dangerous either, Lancelot sniggers.

Perhaps not so dangerous. Even if the final aim was still to free animals from labs and bomb a few things to keep our hand in.

Bomb?

Bomb.

Lancelot scowls. He crosses his arms over his chest, pulling them very tight very high up. Images from one of Irina's documentaries (the first?) come back to him, it was about proboscis monkeys in Borneo dying of malnutrition and thirst because of deforestation. It told the story of two Chinese brothers who destroyed the mangroves to plant oil palms, and shot at the monkeys without making any effort to disguise the pleasure it afforded them. There was a sequence of a mother monkey cradling the remains of her baby and, even though he was dead and dried out like a mummy, still picking parasites off him. Irina cried when she watched that film, tears streaming down her face, even though she herself had filmed it and edited it, and had seen it a hundred times and must have shown it to Lancelot half a dozen times while they were together. She sat on the floor, remote control in hand, and cried. It was as if, every time she watched it, she gave herself an injection of the memory.

Irina didn't drown, Lancelot says.

I know. I've read the autopsy report.

Lancelot feels hollow and empty, he thinks he has drunk something mentholated and acidic which is attacking his insides. I'd like to throw in the sponge, he says to himself.

Who was the man with you the other night? Lancelot asks without looking at Bayer.

What man, which night?

Two nights ago. You weren't on your own. The sound of your conversation woke me.

Bayer turns slowly towards Lancelot as if monitoring his every move in the presence of a dangerous madman. He utters a Huh? making a long slow diphthong of it and stretching his neck forward like a tortoise trying to extricate itself from its shell.

What are you talking about? he blurts.

Lancelot takes a measured breath and stares out at the plane tree with increasing despair.

I feel manipulated, he says carefully.

No no… Bayer reassures him feebly.

I do. I feel manipulated… (He pauses and pulls a face as if swallowing something particularly indigestible. Then goes on:) It's like she sent me to sleep with poisoned drinks and honeyed words…

Bayer does not reply, he seems to be curling up on himself, becoming a closed, grimacing thing. Lancelot watches him shrink and thinks of the palm of a hand closing into a fist.

That's bad, Bayer says eventually.

And Lancelot wonders what he is talking about.

Bayer gets up and goes out, he leaves the door open and Lancelot watches him walk off down the street – scrap-metal merchants and other little houses like Bayer's, the motorway running alongside the suburbs, its multi-coloured sound barriers in dirty plastic just above, swaying slightly and creaking like the branches of an old plum tree. Bayer has put his hands deep into the pockets of his shorts, he is dragging his shoes which are not pulled up over his heels, and his hair drifts about his head like some sort of seaweed. He walks slowly along the pavement. Lancelot remembers that his mother sometimes left the house to go and cry in peace or to stop crying, because her tears dried up of their own accord when there was no audience to be had. Lancelot lets him leave, he stays sitting motionless, cautiously inhaling carbon dioxide and plaster dust from the nearby building site, trying to steady the rhythm of his heart, concentrating on the song of local albino blackbirds. This is his technique, he plays dead.

THIRTY-NINE

On Monday they repair escalators at the airport – several companies share the market between them, and Bayer managed to get a slice of the cake.

They do not talk to each other, and when they get home Lancelot goes straight to his bedroom, not before noticing that Bayer's stool, the one he rests his feet on to contemplate the plane tree at his leisure, has disappeared. Lancelot lies on his bed eating a bar of chocolate, he says to himself, The stool's disappeared, things are contaminated here too, it's nothing to do with me but things still keep vanishing. He would like to confirm this with Bayer but talking to him about such an incongruous subject would look like a clumsy attempt at reconciliation. Bayer is listening to the radio in the next room, and the hiss and click of a newly opened beer can is audible at regular intervals, Lancelot feels on edge and angry like after a domestic row (Can't sleep, it's your fault, your fault, your fault). He lies there, stiff as a ramrod, eyes staring at the ceiling, mulling over his bitterness (the dirty fucker's lying to me, won't tell me anything and won't talk to me). Eventually, completely exhausted, he goes to sleep at about three o'clock in the morning.

On Tuesday they check the goods lifts in the meat market – Bayer does not feel well, he is a vegetarian and being immersed in the horror of barbarities inflicted on animals makes him feel nauseous, he leaves work for several hours, leaving Lancelot to sort out the smaller problems.

They are still not talking. Bayer spends the evening outside.

On Wednesday it is the turn of the reinforced glass lifts in the Saturn tower block.

Lancelot gets two more messages from Marie Marie. He stores them. When he sees that it is her calling, he does not answer. He feels quite unable to speak to her directly. He just stores Marie Marie's messages in his phone's memory with the same obsessive precision which drove him to stockpile Doctor Epstein's blue pills.

Detective Schneider leaves another two messages. She implies she has some information for him, that it would be good if he called her, but Lancelot knows she has nothing to tell him, the second message confirms this conviction, she refers in her iciest voice first to a summons then to an arrest warrant, but Lancelot can tell she feels powerless in the face of his silence. He does not want to talk to her. He would happily crush his mobile with his heel if such a definitive step would not deprive him of Marie Marie's messages.

Lancelot and Kurt Bayer do not exchange a single word through the day on Wednesday. But as they get home that evening, before Lancelot goes and shuts himself in his room, Bayer says, Can I get you anything? Lancelot gives a negative shake of his head and Bayer shrugs his shoulders, It's up to you, he says. An hour later, tormented by the smell of pasta in tomato sauce and by the guilt and satisfaction of letting Bayer make the first move, Lancelot comes out of his room and sits next to Bayer at the table. The latter puts a plate down for him and they eat in silence. Lancelot keeps his eyebrows knitted to ensure there is no ambiguity about a possible over-hasty truce.

On Thursday they repair the escalators at the shopping centre in the Sun Tower, the ones going up to the first floor this time, an intervention made before the place is open to the public, security guards in walking boots, dogs in muzzles, window-cleaners, cleaning women in blue and white overalls like maternity dresses with Peter Pan collars, chatting and joking with Bayer in Spanish, offering him lemon-flavoured sweets and apparently not even noticing Lancelot. He, meanwhile, begins to realize how easily they could blow up each of these temples. There you go, a pack of explosives stashed away under the escalator…

On Thursday evening they go to the supermarket. They fill a trolley with beer and tofu. Lancelot watches the contents of the trolley pile up, shunting the thing around without much conviction. He waits a minute while Bayer chooses an aftershave, opening them one after the other, sniffing them, closing them again, checking the list of ingredients, muttering and putting them back on the shelf.

All right? Lancelot asks eventually.

But Bayer does not reply and carries on with his comparative tests.

Lancelot has to put up with waiting, What else have I got to do, anyway? He adopts a more comfortable position with his arms resting on the trolley and his head hanging limply.

In the end Bayer sets off again and abandons the idea of buying an aftershave. He carries on tossing things into the trolley. They head for the tills. Bayer softens up the checkout girl a bit, her name is Sonia and she laughs without showing her teeth. He pays and they leave.

Bayer drives home, turning on the radio in the car and mumbling to Lancelot, Can you open one for me? so he can drink a beer.

Is there any work tomorrow? Lancelot asks.

Then he thinks, I'm annoying him, I'm actually annoying him, but he doesn't want to say so.

Bayer does not answer. And yet Lancelot senses no hostility in his silence. He surmises that Bayer is not ready to speak. They draw up outside the house and take their shopping out of the boot, it is late and the building site is silent, Lancelot puts the food away on shelves, Bayer drinks another beer and says, Come, follow me.

Lancelot obeys him, the door of the house is left open,

he says, Aren't you going to close it? but Bayer does not reply. They cross the street, then the stretch of wasteland populated by feral cats, they climb down a slope and reach the canal that runs through there. Bayer stands on the bank and throws hunks of stale bread into the water. Round, scaly heads appear. The canal is infested with turtles.

If you fall in, they'll eat you, Bayer warns.

He glances at Lancelot and smiles, angelically.

Why are you feeding them, then?

Bayer carries on breaking up his bread and explains, Because then if I fall in, they won't eat me.

Lancelot nods, not really understanding.

If I keep at it, they might end up vegetarians, Bayer adds.

Lancelot opens his eyes wide but does not want to get any closer. He says:

I can't get over all these turtles… Where are they from?

Bayer leans forward and his only reply is to make a clicking sound with his mouth as if calling them.

The biggest must be a metre across, he says.

Lancelot nods, he watches the turtles' scaly heads, can see the tops of their grey shells emerging above the water, he watches them dive down and resurface, the ones he can see must measure twenty centimetres at the most. They look like tiny, starving ghosts. He thinks to himself, Better keep the door shut at night so they don't come asking for more. I don't want them eating my toes.

The canal is three metres wide, it is choked with weeds,

an upside-down washing machine is rusting a little way away on their right, petrol makes shifting rainbow shapes, the banks are glum and vaguely concreted. Reeds make a clacking sound in the wind with their scalpel-sharp leaves. A willow skims the water with its branches. There is something disheartened about it that Lancelot likes. A yellow cat comes over to the bank and watches the two men and the turtles while it licks its paws and blinks. Lancelot thinks to himself, He understands things I haven't got a clue about.

Bayer smiles as he watches the turtles. When he has run out of bread he lights a cigarette and says, Shall we go back? and cuts back across the wasteland.

Lancelot follows a few metres behind him, head in the air, hands in pockets. He breathes in the evening air and says to himself, I'm OK OK here. He stops, turns round and sees a turtle clambering up onto the side, its clawed feet struggling against gravity. He pictures children coming to set their reptiles free in the canal, encouraging them and jumping up and down on the side. He notices the yellow cat come over, it cuffs the turtle's shell gently with its paw, a delicate, padded batting. The turtle opens its mouth wide as if to grab its attacker. A pink tongue appears from its minute dinosaur's throat. Lancelot thinks to himself, If I were the puddy, I'd try my luck somewhere else. The cat takes an elegant leap backwards, turns away and stalks off with its tail absolutely vertical.

Lancelot stares at the sky, which is going orange in the

west. A chemical orange which whets his appetite. So he starts running (Running? How many years is it since I've run?) and catches up with Bayer before he reaches the house.

FORTY

Who's Paco?

Paco's quite a good sort.

Can you tell me more about him?

He worked in labs for a long time. In a white coat, doing menial tasks, preparing loads of chemical products which had to be sent off and tested in underdeveloped countries.

Labs like Promedan? Romero's labs?

Yes. Among others. Romero tests his crap for curing intestinal cancer and his latest form of contraceptive (a pill once a year) on women in Angola.

So you blew up his house.

Well, at least we managed that, didn't we?

Go on about Paco.

One day he put his oar in. Only a bit, though. He's not the aggressive sort. But he asked one question too many. And he got the boot. With that, his wife left him and took their girls. That was when I met him. He didn't have much left to lose. In the movement we were a bit short of meticulous lab workers in a state of despair.

Then he met Irina.

I introduced her to him.

When was that?

It must have been, what, ten years ago... yes, ten years, or thereabouts.

Ten years...

He became Irina's lapdog. She was a spectacular agitator and that was all he wanted, to be useful to someone like her.

Did they fuck?

Who the hell cares?

I do.

Right. I don't actually think they did. He acted a bit like her protector. It was like she had a permanent loyal bodyguard, to the death. He went with her to Cric meetings, briefed her on everything to do with the chemicals, their destinations, the possible cocktails, at one point I'd had enough of Paco, he was always there, tall and skinny as a spear with a face like an undertaker, never more than five metres from Irina.

Were you still with her at the time?

With her, without her. Never far away, at any rate. I kept my distance after I met Erika, Tralala's mother. I tried to lie low for a bit. Irina was still very active, she started going off to the other side of the world to make her animal documentaries. She carried on being an activist. With Paco in the shadows. He knew how to stand aside when he could tell she didn't want him around. A guy like that can become a drag.

And when she met me?

I imagine she let him know she needed some space.

Do you think he could have wanted to kill her?

Paco? Oh no. You don't know the man. I think he accuses himself of negligence, that yes. At first he thought some sort of organization had eliminated her. Then he told himself she'd just swerved on the bridge and he should have been there to drive her wherever she wanted to go instead of leaving her by herself with all that black ice on the roads.

It was more my job to protect her, wasn't it?

I don't know, Paul. I really don't know. I don't even know where the crap that actually gave her the heart attack was from.

And why Paco Picasso?

Because he obviously doesn't know the other one was called Pablo.

FORTY-ONE

On Friday they do not work. Bayer tells Lancelot to do whatever he likes – Lancelot has never been to pick up his things from the boarding house on the small square with the fire station, he decides against picking up his suitcase but does go back to check his car has not moved, it is still in the same place with its iodine tablets and its lipsticks turning to oil in the glove compartment. He stays there a while, looking at it from a distance, he cannot get over the fact it is still in the same place, things disappear from his field of vision and his whole existence with such regularity that he cannot get over his car still being parked there, he sits down at the wheel, turns on the ignition and decides to leave it in this street, just parked on the opposite pavement so the car pound stays out of it, then he takes a walk around the town, a great languid loop, ending up outside Bayer's red shop where the latter is supposed to be 'busy sorting out paperwork'.

In fact he is not there.

So Lancelot sits out on the terrace of the bar opposite and waits for Bayer to come back.

But he does not.

Lancelot, staying just as calm as if he were still taking Doctor Epstein's pills, sets off for the outskirts of Camerone, towards Bayer's house, he catches a jolting tram which makes such a din of graunching metal you would think there were sparks flying in every direction, and eventually arrives outside the house at the end of the afternoon.

The house is still there.

But the building under construction has gone.

It has been blown up.

Five police cars are flashing in the street, parked any old how along the pavement, as if their arrival was somehow urgent. Lancelot continues on his way. He sees Bayer on his doorstep, smoking and drinking a cup of coffee, placidly contemplating the exalted activities of the policemen who will soon come over to see him, make a note of his brand-new name of Klaus Meyer and the date of birth he gives them on the spur of the moment, who will then ask him whether by any chance he heard anything suspect, he will tell them he has only just got home, that he spent the day in his office doing paperwork, that he doesn't really understand what's happened, Could they explain the situation for him? Is this something to do with the mafia or gas pipes messed up by pneumatic drills? The policewoman will smile, and without even realizing it she will notice

Bayer's hair wafting about his head like strips of kelp (somehow akin to a Gorgon, it will be recorded by her brain and will cling like a parasite to her animal mind, she will not be able to do anything about it, will give up), she will say she is not in a position to give him any information at this moment in time, and will walk away with a slight sway of her hips without realizing what is going on.

Lancelot turns round and cuts back across the town to return to his car.

From now on, he tells himself, this is the only habitable place for him.

He rests his head on the steering wheel and retracts himself, he wishes there weren't a single breath of air or a single drop of water left in him, he wishes he were as dry as a packet of ground coffee and could die of mummification.

He turns on the radio.

The news is not good.

PART FOUR

FORTY-TWO

Lancelot thinks of his marriage to Irina as he listens to the world's bad news. It is an exquisite but devastating thought, as if a huge friendly loneliness were patting him on the shoulder inside his old carcass of metal and rubber.

It stops him thinking of Bayer and his dynamite-fest.

Lancelot is still sitting in his car, forehead on hands and hands on steering wheel. He is listening to the radio, to a brief story about the brief life of a girl whose body was found lifeless (dead?) during a rock festival, he listens to analyses of the Middle East situation, he listens to a description of recurrent bad weather in the north of the country and specialists insisting it has nothing to do with climate change, he listens to a doctor warning consumers about using a lipstick sold in hypermarkets which contains ammonia anhydride, Lancelot turns the volume up, he rummages through the glove compartment and, just as the presenter repeats the brand name of the incriminated lipstick (Redder Than Red), Lancelot finds the two Irina kept there, he swallows hard, feels his heart lurch in his ribcage, it seems to be stuck in his gullet, the man on the radio is describing the sudden death which results from slow but sustained absorption of this poison, there is to be a health enquiry, an impending scandal. Lancelot suffers at the hands of his lovely's contradictions, the chief executive of the cosmetics company that put the lipstick on the market talks about the impossibility of zero risk. Lancelot considers this question, he examines it carefully.

He starts the car.

As he drives, he weighs up what needs weighing up about the life he led with his beloved. We spent, what, two and a half, three years together, and most of the time she was off on her jaunts. He thinks about her macrobiotic food and killer lipsticks, her fuel-heavy trips and her TNT-rich activism. He feels aroused and indignant. Which is not like him.

He thinks, I'm going to suffocate. He tells himself, I'm the sort of man who suffocates. Rather incongruously, he now remembers how Irina used to talk about her orgasms, detailing and describing them the way she might have discussed her dreams over breakfast. One day she said, I sometimes have visions when I orgasm. This time it was an open-air gathering with a whole load of people wearing Stetsons. There was like a sea of Stetsons. And no longer being able to live with a woman who could reveal part of herself to him like that – a taste of the things delicately imploding inside her head, every day, a cluster of neurones, with every sneeze, every glass of vodka, every orgasm – is unacceptable.

He drives across town.

He can hear seagulls screeching over the car, there seem to be so many of them that the multitude disturbs him, he glances up, leaning on the steering wheel.

My sweet my tender my treasure

He thinks about the turtles, Those turtles, he tells himself, are going to be eaten by the seagulls, there are too many seagulls here,

My sweet potato

The seagulls look to him like carnivorous beasts with beaks as sharp as dressmaker's scissors, he can hear them fighting, he stops at a red light, no one looks up to watch their murderous ballet, feathers fly above his car, down settles and sticks to his windscreen, he sets off again and says to himself, They're not ordinary seagulls, cormorants perhaps, or a bigger sort of gull, the ones that never land on terra firma or very rarely, I remember laughing when I watched a documentary about them, they landed comp-letely off balance, they were grotesque and pathetic, so I laughed, and Irina, who was there of course, bristled, she said, Oh please, she frowned and said it again, Please,

My princess my hummingbird my sunshine

there are seagulls (or cormorants or whatever they are)

and acacia trees, and passers-by on the cobbled pavements, passers-by who don't know how to make bombs and who worry about the things people should worry about without ever trying to open the little boxes we stow away inside ourselves,

My darling

Sometimes you open the little box and snap it shut again because it's not nice seeing what you put there, it's like a store-room in a house, a place where you dump things that aren't needed but can't be thrown away, a place that's always a mess,

My sweetheart

or, to be more precise, it's stratified chaos, people keep walking, they don't notice the gulls tearing each other's feathers out, It's raining feathers on my bonnet, they close the little box the minute they open it and it's much better like that, wouldn't you say, otherwise we'd all end up making bombs,

My sweetheart

The buildings become more spaced out, tiny gardens appear and sheet-metal outbuildings, sheds for storing spades, pesticides and rakes, sheds you could put a chair in when it happens to start raining, you could sit there, by the door which is usually padlocked, the padlocked door of the sheet-metal house, and it would only take one puff from the wolf, a little wolf would do, for the whole place to fly apart, so you sit there beside the door, sheltered, granted, and the smell of earth drenched by the rain seeps into you so pleasantly,

My sweetheart

Lancelot drives away from the town centre, he would never have thought he could love the outskirts of a town, there are no more seagulls but their feathers litter the bonnet like the remnants of a war, Lancelot sighs,

My sweetheart

he thinks of the time when he was one of those people who thank the coffee machine as they take their steaming cup, Thank you, they say to the machine, and then glance round in embarrassment to check no one heard them thank a machine,

Oh no,

and Lancelot also used to apologize if someone trod on his toes, Irina was perplexed, I'm sorry, he would say when someone bumped into him, but more out of absent-mindedness than submission, Lancelot did not feel subservient, he felt slightly exterior to the world, and Irina would say, That's worrying, it's usually women who apologize all the time, they've got thousands of years of apologies behind them, and Lancelot shrugged his shoulders and Irina was totally seduced, that much is sure, by that shrug.

My ladylove.

Lancelot goes through the suburbs, he has opened his window, he waits at a red light, puts his arm outside, recognizes the song of a wagtail,

Are there wagtails here?

he thinks about turtles, aggressive seagulls and wagtails, for a fraction of a second he imagines the town in the hands of wild animals (their hands?), he smiles, he can already see the smoking debris of the bombed building, the smoke is still very black, struggling to disseminate its particles of glass and concrete into the evening air, he turns into the street where he lives with Bayer, and there the house is, in the shade of the centennial plane tree, Lancelot carries on smiling, he parks and hops out of the car, it may be a clumsy hop but at least it is light and has an indubitable swagger – flouting gravity and defying asphyxia.

FORTY-THREE

The front door is wide open. Probably to facilitate drafts eliminating the dust hanging in the air.

Lancelot stays on the doorstep for a moment. Stunned. Everything has disappeared. The table, the chairs, the battered oven, the fridge covered in postcards held on with magnets, the green lamp that was so ugly, with a manky old carpet ugliness, the alarm clock that tick-tocked its woeful condemnation on top of the vanished fridge. He says to himself, Shit shit shit, it's never been this bad…

He takes a step into the empty room.

All that is left is the television. It is on. Which, when all is said and done, could be rather worrying. Lancelot parks himself in front of the screen, now he is captive, a female presenter appears all in fireproof plastic. How reassuring, having this girl telling him about the weather, about cumulonimbus and strong fronts, about shifting skies and saints days we must not forget to celebrate, she waves her arms as a butterfly trapped in a net would its wings. She is wearing a strange laced-up garment from which swellings of flesh escape, like a trussed joint of pallid meat. Lancelot pulls himself together and can only move away to counter the effects of testosterone. He goes out into the garden. He feels powerless and abandoned. He might do better to stay sitting on the floor in front of the television screen watching the pretty plastic girls flitting about their aquarium, waiting for the authorities to make the connection between Bayer's house and the bombed building, they would send him heavies in white overalls to kick him out of this tumbledown house, they would take him to a place where they treat people like him but Lancelot wouldn't be a pushover, he would put up a fight, he would play the part of the docile patient but he'd damn well set fire to the hospital in no time. In honour of you know who.

Lancelot notices Bayer's van parked a little way away on the other side of the street. He sees the bed-base secured with bungees to the vehicle's roof. So nothing has evaporated. Bayer is just scramming.

Lancelot can see no movement over by the van. So he walks round the house, treading on suffocated dandelions and disintegrating thistles, he pulls his T-shirt up over his nose, the air is hard to breathe. He sees the well and the slab of concrete laid down beside it in the threadbare grass. He goes up to it and leans over the edge. At the bottom he can see a torch sweeping backwards and forwards, and can hear a damp, scraping sound, seashells being crushed, mud being trampled, someone busy doing something. There is no water at the bottom of this well.

Bayer, Lancelot calls into the dark hole.

The light stops still, everything goes silent. Then Lancelot hears Bayer's distorted voice coming up out of the well, calling, Give me a hand. It's like he's taking refuge at the back of a cave, maybe he's setting up a troglodyte anti-missile bunker in the depths of the well. Then Lancelot hears, Pull the rope.

Lancelot does so, it is not too difficult, Bayer has perfected a system with a pulley and counterweights, Lancelot extricates from the well two jerrycans joined together, he unties the rope and passes it back over the edge, watches it tumble like a snake falling into water, then go taut, Bayer carries on with his performance for a while, the light is failing, Lancelot asks no questions, he has a relaxing impression of well-being carrying out these simple movements, it is beginning to get really dark, Lancelot can only see the torch moving about at the very bottom of the well, he waits for Bayer to give two tugs on the rope and he pulls it back up, he now has twelve jerrycans of petrol by the well. Bayer climbs up the metal ladder and resurfaces. He gestures to Lancelot to help him put the cover back on.

I only need three, he says, pointing at the jerrycans, go and put the others in the van. Lancelot arranges the cans on a trolley and crosses the street, breathing calmly, he puts them into the van, We've got our work cut out, he thinks to himself, stowing the cans next to the bicycle, along with the fridge, the ugly green lamp, the table with its legs in the air, and the old cooker, he puts the trolley on top of everything else, We've got our work cut out, Lancelot closes the doors, trying not to get anything caught or make too much noise (a fairly pointless precaution, all that is left in the area is a canal full of turtles and rubble from the building), he turns towards the house and sees Bayer running towards him across the street, Get in, the latter cries, Lancelot can already see a moving light through the window of the house, he hears the sound of exploding glass, thousands of glittering breakages, Get in, Bayer says again, opening the driver's door, Lancelot climbs in beside Bayer but cannot take his eyes off the house which is starting to swell and burn, he feels excited, terrified and happy with a childish sort of glee, I'm eight years old, his eyes are gaping wide, Bayer starts the car, I'm eight and I've got my whole future in front of me stretching out like a great stony slope, I'm on my skateboard and soon I'm going to launch myself over the edge, Bayer puts the van in gear and it leaps forward, he says, We're stopping at the next phone box, I'll wait for you, you get out and call the fire brigade, I don't want the plane tree to end up burning down. Bayer glances over at Lancelot to get the measure of him, he sketches a smile, then concentrates on the road, he turns left, crosses the bridge over the canal and leaves the neighbourhood, Lancelot settles into his seat, he feels ready to sign a peace treaty, an agreement to the death, his longing for reconciliation pulsates through his veins and illuminates his face, he says out loud, We've got our work cut out. Bayer raises his eyebrows.

Lancelot smiles.

And to himself, because he does not yet have the nerve to say it out loud, because he would feel ridiculous but needs this pronouncement in order really to believe in what he is doing now, Lancelot thinks, My *nom de guerre* will be Paul.

Noël Bourcier

Véronique Ovaldé is the author of the novels *The Sleep of Fishes, All Things Shimmering, Generally I Like Men Very Much* and *Kick the Animal Out* (published by Portobello). *And My See-Through Heart* (originally published as *Et mon coeur transparent*) was a bestseller in France, where it won the popular France-Culture *Télérama* prize and was shortlisted for the Prix Femina and the Prix Lilas. She lives and works in Paris.

Adriana Hunter has been working as a literary translator since 1998, and has now translated over thirty books from the French, including Véronique Ovaldé's *Kick the Animal Out* and Agnès Desarthe's *Chez Moi* for Portobello. She lives in Norfolk with her husband and their three children.